THE LAST MARTIN

THE LAST MARTIN

Jonathan Friesen

ZONDER**kidz**

ZONDERVAN.com/
AUTHOR**TRACKER**
follow your favorite authors

ZONDERKIDZ

The Last Martin
Copyright © 2011 by Jonathan Friesen

This title is also available as a Zondervan ebook.
Visit www.zondervan.com/ebooks.

Requests for information should be addressed to:
Zonderkidz, *Grand Rapids, Michigan 49530*

Library of Congress Cataloging-in-Publication Data

Friesen, Jonathan.
    The last Martin / by Jonathan Friesen.
       p. cm.
    Summary: Thirteen-year-old Martin Boyle struggles to break a family curse
after discovering that he has only twelve weeks to live.
      ISBN 978-0-310-72080-5 (hardcover, jacketed)
     [1. Blessing and cursing—Fiction. 2. Emotional problems—Fiction. 3. Family
problems—Fiction.] I. Title.
PZ7.F91661Las 2011
    [Fic]—dc22   2010048275

Zonderkidz is a trademark of Zondervan.

Editor: Kathleen Kerr
Art direction: Cindy Davis
Cover illustration: Antonio Javier Caparo
Cover design: Cindy Davis
Interior design: Ben Fetterley, Greg Johnson/Textbook Perfect

Printed in the United States of America

---

11 12 13 14 15 16 /DCI/ 22 21 20 19 18 17 16 15 14 13 12 11 10 9 8 7 6 5 4 3 2

To Wendy

Yes, you were right.

"A great new story needs a great first line."

Martin Boyle licked the tip of his pen. "Oh, dumb!" He reached for the antibacterial spray resting on his desk, lifted it mouthward, and squeezed the trigger. His face contorted. The stuff tasted terrible. The taste alone could kill — That was it!

Martin grabbed his notepad.

"Why not kill him now? He's in your grasp!" The jackal circled the motionless body. "Or let me do it for you."

The Black Knight kicked the beast and spat. "Everything in me wants to run him through with his own sword." He turned toward the giant stone and stroked its smooth face. From the center of the rock, a light dimmed.

"What's the matter, my lady? Do you not look forward to our union?"

The Black Knight brought the hilt of his sword down onto the rock. The blade flew from the knight's hands and he swung around. "I need him. I need this sickening, unconscious knight to free my bride! I need him to wake up!" He kicked the body, and a faint groan rose from the floor.

The jackal slumped nearer. "So you do believe in prophesies."

The Black Knight paused. "No." He knelt down and grabbed the White Knight's chin. "I've known this boy from birth, and I assure you, he is not pure in heart." He released the prisoner's mud-caked face, stood, and jumped on top of the stone.

"But an heir to the king? Yes, he is that. The only one who bears the name. And if the old words are true, if he alone can free Alia, then his death can wait a little longer—"

"Martin! Come down from that bedroom! Your spaghetti is cold."

"Okay, Mom," Martin whispered. He stared at the page. "White Knight, you're in a heap of trouble."

CHAPTER 1

I WAS BORN DEAD.

Lani adds stupid and scrawny, but my little sister wasn't there. Mom was the only witness and she owns the tale. She loves to tell the story — usually on spaghetti night — of an evil umbilical cord that coiled like a python around my neck. I came out purply-gray. Silent. Still.

Dead.

Dr. Underland's quick hands untangled me. She whacked and squeezed and inflated my limp lungs. But my wrinkled skin turned cold, and soon the doctor conceded to Death. "I'm so sorry." She shook her head, held me up for the light to glimmer off wet, raisined skin. "It's been too many minutes."

Mom pursed her lips and nodded. "Of course it has." For months, Elaina Boyle prepared herself for this moment — the one when disaster would strike. She knew I would die.

"I fear this was meant to be."

Mom always pauses here for dramatic effect. She reaches over the table and tousles my curly hair, hard. My glasses break free from their perch on my nose and fall lens-down into the spaghetti sauce.

Mom doesn't notice. She's in her glory throughout this tragic epic. "Dead. Limp. Lifeless." She perks up. "Another meatball, Martin?"

I grab a napkin and smear lumpy red off my lenses.

"I was certain your birth would be a tragedy," she says.

Dad clears his throat. I sit quietly. Lani can't.

"It was!" She grins and sneezes.

"Would you be quiet?" I say.

Mom lunges over the table and snatches up our centerpiece, a soap-filled gravy dish surrounded by fake fruit. A minute later, Lani is lathered and cleansed. Mom breathes deeply and continues. "Maybe if your father had been around — " She shoots Dad a sharp glance. His garlic toast pauses halfway between plate and mouth, then finishes the trip.

"Had he been home, I wouldn't have needed to find *my own way* to the hospital. Oh, the stress. You could have lived."

"But I did live!"

"Yes, I know." She looks at me and sighs. "Such a strange day that was. Cheese, anyone?"

Mom's in no hurry to retell the rest. But it's Dad's favorite part, so it's my favorite too.

The doctor placed my tiny carcass on Mom, and she cried — big, fat Mom tears. Three minutes later, she launched into her what-a-dangerous-world-this-would-have-been speech. It must have been a stirring version because I hiccupped. Again. And again. Then I coughed.

Mom sniffled and sat up. "What's happening?"

Dr. Underland dropped her clipboard and rushed toward the bed. "Touch him! Rub him. Your son is trying to live."

Mom lifted up my arm and let it flop back down. "Can't be happening."

It took a while for me to convince her, but by evening I had earned "miracle child" status, and Mom was overjoyed. As was Dad.

He burst into the newborn nursery the next day, fresh from the airport and still wearing his army fatigues. He grabbed the first child he saw, raised him to heaven, and christened him Martin, Martin Boyle. The child already had a name — Ahmad — and this caused quite a commotion. A husky nurse yanked the double-named brown kid from Dad and pointed to the bluish boy in the corner. Dad said he'd never been so proud.

He scooped me into strong arms, as every firstborn male born into the Boyle clan has been scooped. He spoke the words every firstborn Boyle has heard:

"I name you Martin."

And for the first time in my brief life, I cried.

"Train!"

I drop my fork with a clink. Mom's holler inter-rupts her own spaghetti story, and she scurries over to the cowbell that hangs above the kitchen sink. Lani and I cover our ears.

Dong.

Mom sounds the alarm. Children beware. Get off the tracks, a train rumbles near.

She feels them coming deep in her bowels. I'm not sure where exactly that is, but her saying the b-word makes me squirm.

Of course, there are no children on the tracks, but Mom says she sleeps better knowing she did her part.

"What if?" She points to the three of us in turn. "What if there had been children at play on the rails? And they were deaf or dead? And the railmen fell asleep and rounded the bend?" She folds her arms and raises eyebrows in victory. "What would you say then?"

Lani shrugs. "Deaf kids couldn't hear your bell and dead ones don't need to?"

Mom puffs out air, plops down in her chair. "But my conscience is clear."

Clearly disturbed. Clearly paranoid. So yeah, clear.

But Mom's right about one thing. There are trains. Lots of them. House rattlers that rumble so near our home, the glasses tinkle in the cupboard.

It's what comes from living In Between, in the no-man's-land between downtown and the suburbs. It's an odd middle place filled with steel factories and smokestacks and train yards. It's where the Burlington line tires of heading north, hangs a U-ey, and heads west. And in the middle of the concrete and steel stand six old houses, built before there was concrete or steel. Huge houses that don't belong.

"Still," Mom continues, "train infestations are safer than animal infestations. In that regard, you're safe as safe can be," Mom says. "Surrounded by activity, out of the city, near a hospital, and far from the *wilderness*."

She fires Dad another harsh look. This time he sets down his fork and folds his hands. His cool eyes catch Mom off-guard, his words slow and carefully chosen.

"I can't help it my brother and Jenny chose to live in the *country*." He glances around the table. "Don't worry. It's not for another week, and we won't stay long." He lowers his voice, so that I think only I hear. "Hate to see you mauled by a squirrel."

"Can't Martin and I stay with Uncle Landis while you two go to the cemetery?" Lani squirms. "All those dead bodies — "

"Yeah." I bite my lip. "We could wait for you both at the farmhouse. I never met those buried people anyway."

Mom pushes back from the table. "Do you hear them, Gavin? The children are terrified and for good reason. They understand that cemeteries are breeding grounds for germs and — "

"No." Dad stands, and his eyes flash. "We will all go — Lani, without your attitude; Martin, without your fantasy books; and please, Elaina — without your paranoia."

Dad whips his napkin onto the table and storms down the stairs to Underwear World.

It's silent until Mom clears her throat. "Don't worry. I'll talk to your father."

I can't look at her. If Dad walked up, I couldn't look at him either.

So much for making him proud.

CHAPTER 2

I GROAN, STRETCH, AND WHACK THE SNOOZE BUTTON. Curtains hide the morning, but I feel it — it's April. Today even Industrial Boulevard, the service road that leads to our chunk of In Between, will feel springy. There'll be warm sun and warm smiles and nobody at school will understand. But the April flowers lining the sidewalk? They know. They smile all innocent, but from their roots rise a mocking mutter, "Woe to you, Martin. Your time is near."

I'm six days from D-Day. Dead Day.

I collapse onto my back and bury myself beneath covers.

My mind fills with life's little horrors: The smile of wicked Dr. Devlin, a dentist who doesn't believe in happy gas; the pierce of Lani's fish hook, cast into my left nipple. Then there was our one camping trip — poison oak leaves certainly look like suitable toilet paper.

Painful, yes. Terrifying, no.

Our family's yearly pilgrimage to honor the Boyle dead wins the creepiness award hands down.

I squeeze my knees to my chin — turn into a tiny Martin ball — and feel a pit, not a tiny grape pit, but a big old avocado pit, roll around my gut. I'm thirteen, they're not breathing, and I shouldn't have to hang around them.

And I'm not laying my hand on Great-Grandpa Martin's stone. Not this year.

"Wake up, sleepyhead!"

Cripes. The Barn Owl. Mom's song rises through the vent, wriggles under my blanket, and slaps me on the cheek. I exhale hard.

Maybe it wasn't kind of Lani to nickname Mom after a carnivore that feeds on mice, but so be it. Mom sees all, moves silently, and never sleeps.

I roll off the bed and thump against the hardwood. Pages from my fantasy story flutter down like flowers at a funeral. I gather up the story and stuff it in the desk drawer. No time to shower. I throw on balled-up clothes and fight a comb through cowlicked brown hair. My reflection scowls back at me from the computer screen.

"Einstein. On a bad hair day." I stumble out my door and down the stairs.

"Good morning, Martin. Martin, good morning. Whoo, whoo, whoo, whoo — "

My feet grind to a halt, and my chest tightens.

Morning people should never sing-hoot at people before 8:00 a.m.

"Come off those steps, my dear." Plates clatter in the sink. "You're late. You'll need to eat breakfast on the way."

"Um, hmm." I creak onto the main floor, peek into the kitchen. "Where's Lani?"

"Sick." Mom glances over her shoulder, sighs, and approaches. She licks her palm and works her spit through my Einstein hair. Not only germy, but really second grade and really gross. "Your sister sneezed twice last night."

I swat at Mom's hand and grab my backpack from the floor. "Wait, I need to say bye to Dad."

Mom pauses. "He left hours ago. His regiment has another battle reenactment at Fort Snelling. I don't expect him home until mid-week." She digs in the closet for my jacket. "When Gavin retired from the service, I thought we'd placed this schedule behind us. But I declare, the demands of a Living History Museum are equally intolerable. Guns blazing, crude talking, chew spitting, and sleeping with bugs. It is utterly amazing that man is still alive."

Inside, I feel it. A little flutter. It frightens and excites me at the same time.

"Do you think someday he'd take me with him? It'd be like school. It's history, right? I mean, those battles really happened."

Mom's hands shoot to her hips, my jacket clenched in her fist. "I will not have you missing the important lessons of life — the writing of haiku or perhaps new techniques of proper hygiene ..." Her arms drop and her voice softens. "Your father is a good man, but he lives in the past, and — " She places her hand on her abdomen, strains her ear toward the door. "Your bus is here. Run!"

I scoot outside, skip down porch steps, and dash for the yellow speck in the distance.

Only eight kids live near the Midway district of St. Paul, not enough to deserve a real school bus. We get the shrunken version — special-ed. transportation. It's hard to feel self-confident when your bus is the size of a minivan.

I reach the accordion door, double over, and suck air. My thighs burn and I blink and wince and stare up the steps of the bus at our driver's smiling face. Father Gooly is the size of a minivan too. The priest is a mountain, dressed black as night, with a little snow cover on his collar beneath both chins. All around, belly-fat foothills overflow his seat.

"Top of the mornin' to you, Martin! Comin' aboard, or would you be taking the wheelchair ramp in?"

"No, thanks." I step up and squeeze by those blubbery hills. "I'm good."

The bus smells like flu. That dreadful combination of sick room plus 7-Up plus soda crackers. I hold my breath and shuffle down the aisle.

So much for April fresh.

I run out of air, take several shallow breaths, and scan for Charley. My gaze falls on Brooke, my nearest neighbor. She rolls her eyes, sets her backpack beside her to fill the seat, and points her thumb back over her shoulder. I smile and push by her and stare down at my pasty-faced best friend.

"What's wrong?" I plop into place, door hinges squeal, and we jerk forward. "You look sick." My rear inches away from Charley.

"I'll wait 'til you're finished," he says.

I nod and go to work. I remove the portable air bag from my pack, stick both arms through the straps, and tighten the belt at my chest. Mom bought the contraption from the Sky Mall, a bargain at $149.99. According to the ad, I'm now perfectly safe from ninety percent of possible traffic accidents.

"I need your help in English." Charley glances over at me, his face all droopy. "I promised her I'd write the story if she'd be my partner and do the illustrations."

"Her?"

My friend — my *best* friend — bites his lip and frowns. "Well come on, Marty. You're never going to talk to Julia."

My voice gets quiet. "I was going to talk to her today."

"About what? She plays lacrosse. She rides four-wheelers. She's into crazy stuff and outdoor stuff. Camping, fishing—"

"I fished once." My nipple twitches, and I reach up to massage my chest. "You know I tried that." I hold my breath, turn away, and sigh. "What's your story for English about?"

Charley straightens, flops a pad and pen onto my lap. "Okay, it's supposed to be a fairy tale based on a real-life event. So anything, you know? Some dumb prince, princess deal."

"Have a start?"

He chews some more on that lip and gives a quick nod. "There." Charley points at the paper.

"'A Prince and a Princess,' by Charley Baxter." I look over at him. "How long did that take?"

"Most of Saturday."

"Right." I close my eyes, think of Julia, twiddle the pen around in my hand, and settle into my seat. "I started a new story. I'll write one page for you to use, but that's it."

"I tire of waiting. I'll do this myself." The Black Knight lifted the sword, its tip glinting in the torchlight. His minions—

Charley grabs my arm. "What's a minion? That like an onion?"

I yank free. "His bad guys."

His minions lurched forward. Sweat traced down beneath their armor, fell in black pools on the stony ground of the prison where the White Knight and the princess were held captive.

"Cursed White Knight, behold the end of your dream. This dungeon is your destiny. And now Alia is mine. Yah!" The sword fell upon the clear stone with a clank. Sparks flew through the air. Fire rained upon the Black Knight's helmet.

"My sight!" He reeled, clawed at his eyes, and stuck his finger in the White Knight's chest. "It is true! The prophecy. Only one pure of heart can free the beauty trapped within the crystal." He gestured around the room. "Guards, loose the man!"

Hideous creatures, black of heart and mind, crushed the shackles that bound the White Knight's hands and feet, and he slowly rose. Silently, he approached the stone and gazed down into it. His love gazed up from within the rock. Such pure crystal. Had Alia made it so? Her smooth features radiated light from within. She looked so at peace—save for her eyes. They beckoned to him, and he could not free himself from the call. Would she ever know how he felt? Would she ever know his secret? He would live forever trapped in a dark and lonely world, forever far from her, but she would be free. He would do this much.

"The sword," he whispered.

The Black Knight reached down, grasped the sword, and thrust him the grip. "Ere you do this, know that when she is free, she will be mine."

Sadly, the White Knight laid hold of the shaft, raised it to heaven, and—

"Yow!" Charley grabs the pencil from my hand. "Why'd you jab me? What'd I do?"

I blink hard and wipe sweat from my forehead. "Sorry. I just got carried away."

Charley snatches the pad away from me. "I'll finish—"

Tires screech and the bus swerves.

"Spring pothole!" Gooly hollers.

Front tires drop a foot into the earth. We lurch into tar, and my world explodes. It's a balloon, or an angry marshmallow, but it thunders against my face and chest like a buffalo and pins me to my seat.

"Martin blew up! Martin blew up!" Girls scream and feet pound down the aisle.

"White guts!"

"Everyone out," Gooly huffs. "Slow down, Brooke, easy now. I'll see to the lad."

"Charley," I whisper. "You okay? Charley?"

I walk my fingers along the seat. No friend.

Charley gets out, the White Knight explodes. Figures.

Fifteen minutes later, I'm still pinned. The fire department finally arrives and extracts Father Gooly, wedged in the aisle, and then deflates my protective device.

"My son needs me." Outside, Mom's voice cuts through the murmurs. "Bring him out this instant!"

I stare at my rescuer, a muscular fireman with a thin mustache. "If I give you my lunch money, any chance you'd sneak me to Fort Snelling?"

"Sorry, kid." He checks my neck, pauses to listen to Mom rant. "Your mom is pretty upset."

"Not really. She lives for disasters."

Minutes later, my fire guy removes his helmet and lifts his hands. "You, young man, have a clean bill of health. Let's get you to your mom before *she* explodes."

He turns away, and I panic — don't know why but I panic — and I grab his sleeve and tug. "Do you believe in fairy tales? I mean, like the happy ending parts even if they look *totally* and *probably* impossible, and you might not even know what a happy ending looks like because for thirteen years all you felt was stuck — maybe stuck on the inside and definitely stuck on the outside and legally the stuck will last five more years, but even then you'll probably stay stuck because you've been stuck for so long you don't know any other way to live? Do you believe in happy endings anyway?"

He tongues the inside of his jaw and scratches his head. "Yeah. Reckon I do."

I smile. "Me too."

"Stuck?" The Barn Owl screeches at a policeman.

"My son is not stuck. I see him plain as day, speaking with that fireman. What is taking so long?"

My rescuer shakes his head and glances out the window. "She's a piece of work."

I exhale hard. "I know."

CHAPTER 3

MOM KEEPS ME HOME FOR THE REST OF THE WEEK —
a twisted house arrest during an unseasonably
warm stretch of spring. She frowns whenever I venture
out of my room.

"You shouldn't take chances with PTSD." Mom
insists she saw Pothole Traumatic Stress Disorder fea-
tured on an early episode of Oprah, and for her, that
seals the matter.

"Oh Martin, if you could have seen the panel of suf-
ferers. They were visibly shaken." She shoos me up the
stairs. "Now, I've taken a week off from the library to
care for you. Don't push it."

I drop the phone onto the sofa and trudge back up
to my cell. "Fine. I just wanted to see Charley, is all." My
voice lowers to a whisper. "I'll be up here if you need me.
In my room. Watching the trains go by."

"Up, Martin!"

I crack an eyelid and jump to my feet. My new copy of *Dragon's Revenge* thunks onto the floor.

"Dad! You're home." My gaze wanders over his uniform, bloody and threadbare.

"Shoes on. In the car in five minutes."

I reach down, grab my book, and set it on the desk. "But Mom said—"

The heel of Dad's musket pounds the floor. "Have you or have you not been in this house for four straight school days because your bus popped a tire?"

"Well, I mean ... yeah." I risk a look into his eyes.

Dad nods big and slow. "Elaina, my dear," he whispers, "you have a crossed a line."

I eye the gun. "That's not loaded, is it?"

"Five minutes, in the car. You're going to school."

Classes have ended for the day, and we pull in as buses load. Shrieks and laughter, running kids, and helpless teachers line the front of Midway Middle School. Sure it's April and we have months of education left, but when the snow vanishes, everyone knows it's all over.

Dad squeals into the visitor-parking space, throws open the door, and strides toward the school. I don't move—a fact he doesn't notice for a good twenty paces. He stops and gives an exaggerated point, straight down.

I shake my head. Not before the buses are gone.

I don't mind walking with Dad. In fact, there's no place I'd rather be. I do mind walking beside a United States soldier dressed in the finest 1820 had to offer, and smelling the part.

Behind Dad, kids hang from buses. They laugh and point at the bloodstained kook in the parking lot.

But Dad hollers my name — I hear it through the glass — and I breathe deeply.

Just keep the eyes down and the ears closed.

I step out, stare at tar, and shuffle forward. I'm not mad at him — don't know that I have it in me. My stomach turns because of Mom. She's the one who kept me home. She's the one who's lost it. Mom is the one with crazy juice that surges through her brain and yanks her into an alternate paranoid universe. And it's not enough for her to live there alone; now she's injected the poison into Lani and me, and I know the only reason she doesn't seem totally nuts is because we're infected too.

"Hey, Martin, who's the other crazy?"

I wince and ignore Will Chambers' voice. *He doesn't know my dad.* We reach the glass doors. *He doesn't know anything.*

The soldier and I march into the office. We get prompt service.

"Martin?" Ms. Corbitt, the secretary, lowers the rims of her glasses to peek at my escort. "And you are ..."

"Gavin Boyle. I'd like to speak to Principal Creaker."

Ms. Corbitt rises and motions to a chair. "He's out doing dismissal, but you may certainly wait for him there."

I turn and slump into molded plastic. Dad stands beside me, my own personal sentry.

It's not long before Creaker hobbles into the office. The man is old. Noah old. Knotted, bony fingers. Nose and ear hair that need combing. It's a miracle he's not resting in some ark beneath the ground. I catch my breath, think of Great-Grandpa Martin walking upright, and feel a chill.

"Come in, Mr. Boyle. Martin."

Dad smiles for the first time today, reaches down, and hauls me up by the arm.

We enter the principal's office, and Creaker collapses into his chair with a groan. "This feels good." He gestures toward Dad. "You know, there's a fairly good chance I fought in that battle."

Dad's out of smiles, and Creaker purses his lips and sighs. "You were gone, Gavin. She came straight on in and said she was keeping the boy home." He shakes his head. "It's her right."

"I've spoken to her already." Dad runs his hand through his hair. "What reason did she give?"

Creaker digs in his drawer and pulls out a thick file labeled *Martin Boyle*. "She put it in a note." He hands a crisp sheet to Dad, who mumbles aloud.

To whom it may concern:
Seeing as Martin Boyle has experienced
emotional strain and physical duress due to
PTSD...

Dad opens his palm. "What's that?"

I lean over and whisper, "Pothole Traumatic Stress Disorder."

Dad looks at me and chuckles. "Ah yes." He clears his throat, continues,

PTSD, and his father is once again absent for
consultation...

Dad glances toward the principal. "No phones in 1820, you see."

"Ah yes." Creaker grins.

"Okay," Dad skims. "Where was I? Oh, here."

... absent for consultation, I feel it best to at-
tend personally to his needs. I, therefore, will
be keeping Martin Boyle home from school for
the remainder of the week.

Sincerely,
Elaina Boyle

It's quiet.

"Well," Dad says, and slowly sets the paper on the desk. "We can't make up those days. But you can be certain that Martin will be in school tomorrow."

The principal rises and creaks toward a file cabinet. "No, he won't."

I blink hard.

"We have a staff in-service. There's no school on Friday." He grabs a thick manila envelope. "But I've gathered work from all Martin's teachers. I've no doubt that come Monday, he won't be far behind."

Ten minutes later we pull into our driveway, and the soldier rubs his forehead. "This isn't your fault, Martin." He looks toward the house. "Much of it's mine."

I shrug, open my door, and pause. "I was thinking. Since I missed so much schoolwork, it'd probably be best if I skipped the graveyard ceremony this year to make it up."

"No." Dad squeezes my shoulder. "I don't care about what's in the principal's envelope. I'm more worried about you. So tomorrow, we'll be spring-cleaning around here, and Saturday, *we're* heading up north."

5:00 a.m. Friday morning. I sneak into the study, nestle into Dad's chair, and stretch my fingers. Before the day starts and the world gets crazy, my mind is still and clear. There's no better time to work on *The White Knight*.

The knight remembered his last visit to the citadel. Strange, there had been no sentry. The silence hung heavy, and he shielded his eyes and gazed toward the turret. No trumpeter announced his arrival; no cheers greeted the son home from battle. The place that should be his comfort felt foreign.

All he wanted was his father's approval, but the king was not there—

Lani throws open the doors. "Ditch the story. Barn Owl alert."

"Spring-cleaning!" Mom's voice echoes through the home.

I run my epic upstairs, dash back down. The others are assembled in the family room.

"Kids," Dad stares from Lani to me and back again. "You know your tasks. We have one day this year—I want the work completed before tomorrow's trip." His gaze falls on me. "Begin."

He spins and marches downstairs to do battle with the basement. Mom and Lani squeeze into rubber gloves and protective masks to disinfect the house, and I push out the back door, walk to the shed, and grab the green paint. It's my job to paint the garden.

Germ-infested dirt makes a real garden out of the question. But there is the boxcar, the one parked on the abandoned track that splits our backyard in two. It's the freakiest part of living here, with its gaping mouth, damp, black interior, and graffiti-covered sides.

On spring-cleaning day, the train car gets a fresh coat of forest green. Once dry, I'll paint the flowers and lastly some tomato plants. I'd once painted a spring-time pumpkin, but being out of season, it didn't sit too well.

"Where you been all week?" Charley runs up from behind. He always walks over on spring-cleaning day to watch my tomato art.

I don't look at him. "This boxcar gets bigger every year."

"I just read this book, forgot the title, but this mouthy kid had to paint a whole fence and I didn't see him complaining."

"See that graffiti?" I point with my brush. "Takes talent."

"It also says PYUKE. I can see why your mom wants it painted."

"Well then." I drop my brush into the green paint bucket. "Since you brought up *Tom Sawyer*, did mouthy Tom paint that fence? Nope. He didn't. His friends did." My toe nudges the can. "So go ahead." I puff out steam. "And don't tell me you read that book. You don't read anything."

Charley picks up the brush and soon the P and the E are covered in green. "There. YUK." He looks down.

"Okay, Julia read *The White Knight* in English class. She's talking to me all the time since ..."

I glare at my betrayer.

He runs his hand through his hair. "... since my story, er, your story ..." Charley glances around. "I need to know what happens next." He peeks at me and raises both hands. "Last favor. Last one ever. She's been waiting on me and all week I've been waiting on you and if I don't come up with the next installment of *The White Knight* soon, she'll know."

"That you're an idiot."

He shrugs. "Basically."

I pick up the brush and paint furiously.

"Talk to me here. You don't even need to write it down." He sticks his arm in front of my face. "I'll pretend I sprained my wrist and tell her the next part."

"No!"

"Help your friend out," a voice echoes from inside the boxcar. "It'll make you feel worse."

We jump back, and the owner of the voice pokes his head out and stares at me. "Give Charley some assistance."

Charley grabs my arm. "You keep a kid in there?"

"Oh yeah, like I knew." I swallow hard. *This kid's been hiding in my backyard!* I cock my head to get a better look at his. "How long have you been ... I mean, what are you ... who ..."

The head disappears, and a second later, an entire body leaps into view. Limber like a leprechaun, the boy lands lightly and dangles his legs out over the edge.

I'd put him about my age, I think, but there's nothing distinctive about him. Except for grime. There's plenty of that on his tanned face. Plenty more on callused hands. It's the kind of grime that likes clothes as much as skin, and it covers baggy tan railroad trousers and a plaid, button-down shirt, half untucked.

The kid's strong — tall and wiry, my grandpa would have said — it's clear from the way he moves. I guarantee he'd whip me in a race, a fight, or any competition involving germ count.

"My name's Poole, and I've been here long enough to know you well. And your sister. There's the Barn Owl and the Sergeant and, of course, your friend Charley." He leans back and spreads his arms. "I know everyone on my line. I know them all." The boy leans forward, the grin vanishes, and he stares into me. "But I especially know you, Martin."

His gaze reaches someplace I don't want it to go, but I can't break free. Not sure I want to. His eyes blaze like Dad's do when Mom gets too loopy. I didn't think anybody else could look that intense.

I try to run, but my legs stick, my mouth dries, and my mind blanks. I peek at my buddy, who wears a face I've never seen on him before. Forget dumb Charley. My poor friend is confused times ten, with a hint of terror rounding out the look.

Get help!

"You stay right there." I point back over my shoulder. "I need to get into that house." I back away from the kid — the one who popped out of my backyard boxcar. "Don't. Move. A muscle. When my mom sees you — "

"No problem, Marty. Enjoy tomorrow. Heck, enjoy today while you're at it." Poole nods, leaps out into my yard, and stretches. "What a beautiful day!"

"You moved!" I race inside, slam the door behind me, and breathe deeply.

"I was just going to call you in." Mom strides up and picks a fleck of green off my cheek. "Aren't you well? Too much fresh air, no doubt."

"Right now. Outside. Grimy kid … Just look outside. At the garden. What are they doing?"

"They?" Mom peeks out the window. "There's nobody there … wait." She presses her nose to the glass. "I declare, why is Charley doing your work?"

"Doing my work?"

Mom purses her lips and shakes her head. "It certainly isn't his."

"You're sure it's Charley?" I back toward the stairs, stumble over an end table, and regain balance. I don't want to look.

"Who else would it be?"

"Right." I pound up the steps, run to my window, and peek out. I don't see a soul. Because there wouldn't be anyone else. There's only a creepy boxcar playing creepy tricks on a creeped-out mind.

Dad's right. Maybe one too many fantasy books.

CHAPTER
4

"DRESS QUICKLY." DAD RAISES MY SHADE. "WE LEAVE in fifteen minutes."

I glance at the window and watch beads of rain race down the pane. I can't push the day away. It has come.

I dress slowly, step into the hall, feel its chill, and pause. "Farewell bedroom, my cozy, comfortable friend."

Downstairs, Mom has packed. Three bulging suitcases rest near the door.

She stares, arms folded, and squints at the largest.

Dad rolls his eyes, glances at me, and points toward the smallest piece.

I crack my knuckles, double-fist the handle, and yank. Both shoulders pop. "That hurt. That really hurt." I wince and rub, peek at Dad and tug again. "This thing's heavy—"

"Psst!" Mom raises a finger, regains her frown, and continues her mutter. "Gauze. Knee braces. Aspirin.

Your breakfast is on the table, Martin. Face masks. Rubber gloves ..."

I back away. I'm not hungry.

Dad's hand lands heavy on my disjointed shoulder. "The day we've been waiting for, eh, son?" He gestures toward the door with his head. "I'll take care of her bags, but you left two paintbrushes in the backyard yesterday. Quick go pick them up and we're off."

Technically, it was Grimy and Charley that used 'em last, but ... I reach for the door.

"... alcohol scrubs, wet wipes, put on your rain jacket and boots, tweezers, inhalers ..."

I grab my duck-yellow rain slicker and wet-boots and slip outside. It's a hard, straight-down rain and puddles, like tiny lakes, cover half of the yard.

Okay, brushes, where are you — oh no.

One rests in the mouth of the boxcar.

I bite my lip and whisper, "I do not want to see Grimy Boy who knows me and knows my family. Did I give him permission to borrow Dad's stern face? No, I did not."

"Poole?" I clear morning from my throat and creep ahead. My boots slow to a stop in the middle of the yard. "You aren't in there, are you?"

Nothing.

"That's good, because you make me nervous and you don't pay us rent and you probably don't go to school or change underwear or take showers which makes you a walking germball." I swipe wet from my forehead. "And all those are very, very good reasons for you to live elsewhere."

I tiptoe forward, wincing with each loud squish of my boots. Rain drums off the top of the train, the echo pounding out its gaping mouth. I stop an arm's length away.

Droplets fall from my trembling hand, and I stretch for the brush bristles. I grasp them, squeeze them, watch the slick paintbrush squirm free and land at my feet with a splash.

"Quiet already!" I hiss at my fingers. "For once, will you please cooperate?"

A second paintbrush whistles out from the darkness of the boxcar and narrowly misses my head.

"Ah!" I gasp, grab the brush at my feet, and race toward the house. My foot slips on ghost brush number two, and my butt lands hard in muck. I scramble to vertical. My heartbeat pounds in my eardrums, and I burst through the front door, a brush clenched in each smeary brown fist.

"My goodness, Martin." Mom recoils. "What on earth —"

"I ran. I fell. I got up. Brushes!"

Slap. They drop into Dad's big hands. Lani leans over and looks at my rear end.

"Ew! Know what that looks like?"

Dad tousles my hair. "A little mud never hurt anyone. My unkempt appearance was what first drew your mother to me." He shoots a glance at my pursed-lip, slit-eyed, red-cheeked mom. "We're late," Dad continues. "Let's load up."

Our Suburban ventures north and leaves the safety of smokestacks and four-lane highways. I sit with my worries. Behind me, a paintbrush-flinging homeless boy lives in my garden. Before me, rotting bones of dead men await. And all the while Charley uses my brain to wriggle closer to Julia. Life is officially horrible.

Lani sits to my left, hands folded, and stares out the window. She's a picture of Mom. Erect, alert, watchful. After all, one never knows what we'll encounter in the wilderness. A deer? A vagrant?

"You must be careful for vagrants. Stay vigilant, children." Mom scans from side to side. "The further one strays from civilization, the nearer you are to the world of desperate savages. I tell you, the wilderness destroys rationality."

Dad coughs and waggles his head; cranks his seat back further. He smiles the contented smile I only see once a year — on Grandparent's Day, the day we enter the land of vagrants.

I lean over, tap Lani, and whisper, "What are you staring at?"

She rolls her eyes. "Mom put me on backseat vagrant alert."

I nod. "Seen any?"

"Only trees."

I straighten, then lean over again. "I saw somebody in our backyard. In the boxcar."

"A vagrant? Don't tell Mom. She'll freak." Lani peers out her window. "I don't want to hear about it either." She peeks at me. "What did he look like?"

"Honest?" I whisper, and slump down in my seat. She slumps too. I point at my rear, at the dried mud. "Mud. Mud everywhere. About my age too. Inside our garden train crawls one grimy vagrant." I raise my eyebrows and give an exaggerated nod.

Lani smirks. "Yeah, sure. Earth to Smeary Butt. Like we couldn't tell who was crawling around in there."

"*Me*? Do you think I'd go in there with *him*? It's probably the kid's summer home. Look behind my beautifully painted tomato plants and you'll find a homeless genius who knows everything about everyone. Freaky."

She clears her throat. "A brilliant boy in our backyard."

"Yep. He probably reads our mail and peeks in our windows. That's it. That's where he saw Dad's stare. Grimy must have seen it and practiced it and then he used it on me and Charley."

Lani bites her lip. "So ... today you saw a strange kid appear from inside the boxcar — "

"No. Today I saw nothing, unless you count the ghost brush. The kid whipped it at my head. Yesterday was the day vagrant boy nailed me and Charley with the look, you know?"

"So, of course you told Mom."

"Tried to, but the kid's quick. Or maybe he hides in tunnels beneath the train. Beneath the yard. Beneath our house."

Lani is silent for a few seconds. "I got it. It's very clear now." She straightens, faces me, and puffs out air. "You're stuck in a fantasy story. Let me help you, Martin. You live on planet Earth, Dad still owns his eyeballs, and there is no vagrant growing in our garden!"

"Lani!" Mom turns to Dad. "I trust you're pleased. The children are falling apart before our eyes. Blubbering and screaming fits. This will take weeks to set right, mark my words."

"Your words are marked, my dear." Dad breaks into a whistle — "The Battle Hymn of the Republic."

We turn onto a windy gravel road, just wide enough for one vehicle. Ten miles later, gravel turns to washed-out mud. Dad throws the Suburban into four-wheel drive and we plow ahead.

"There it is, everyone." Dad slows at an oversized mailbox and stares at a break in the woods. "Remember?"

As if we could forget. Uncle Landis and Aunt Jenny live at the end of this ... driveway.

"They are aware that we're coming?" Mom's hard face cracks and her voice wavers.

Dad reaches over and rubs her tight neck. "I sure hope so."

Uncle Landis doesn't know. He can't. He has no phone. No landline, no cell phone. They have no computer, no television. They are isolated from the world. Dad calls them survivalists, but it seems a sure way to get yourself killed. If a bear attacks, hollering "9-1-1" doesn't cut it.

Yep, Uncle Landis loves three things: his Jenny, his privacy, and his guns, which stand at the ready in every room — including the bathroom. And it's hard to do business with the toilet paper roll jammed onto the end of a loaded weapon.

All that weirdness on the other end of this driveway.

Dad backs up, floors it, and we leave the world. Mom flips the all-door lock toggle, and we spin forward. Behind us, mud kicks high into the sky, and the Suburban angles left.

"Not good." Dad winces. "Hang on." He cranks the

wheel with no effect and we slosh to a stop, our tires eaten by a foot of heavy-duty mud. Dad runs his hand through his hair. "Boyle Company, prepare to march."

"Most certainly not." Mom reaches back and holds her hand in front of our faces. "Stay here, children. Your father will go for help."

Dad opens his door, pauses, and closes it again. "You want to come with me, Martin?"

"Outside?"

"Yes, out — Whoa!"

Dog face mashes against the windshield, and the pit bull hurls his body against the glass. He bares his fangs, barks with full throat, and oozes foam. He's clearly fresh from a kill and hungry for more.

I'd forgotten about Tripod, the three-legged terror.

Dad laughs and squirts him with wiper fluid — it has no effect on the already soggy beast. But the wipers catch him across the neck and he recoils, hypnotized by the back-and-forth motion of the blades.

"Are you coming, Martin?" Dad reaches back and slaps my shoulder.

I point at the dazed creature. "It might be best if I stay with Lani."

Dad looks into me and sighs. I sigh too. Because something inside me wants to throw open my door. Not to watch Tripod sink teeth into my thigh — I could skip that part — but to be on the same side of the glass as

Dad. To look back at Mom's terrified face. That view would almost be worth the stitches.

"Hey!" Lani points. "We're saved!"

A huge tractor chugs toward us with Uncle Landis sitting high. Tripod leaps off the Suburban and scampers beside him. Moments later, Dad and Landis exchange backslaps, drop to the mud, and stretch chains from our vehicle to Landis's rig.

"That should do it!" Dad hops back in, ten shades muddier and a good deal cheerier. The Suburban jerks forward and plows through mud to the farmhouse.

Mom turns toward Lani. "Vagrants."

Dad glances over his shoulder. "Family."

The rain has stopped. We ease out. From the porch, the screen door slams and Aunt Jenny waddles toward Mom.

"So good to see all of you. Elaina, you look wonderful." She wipes bloody drippings onto her apron and clasps Mom's hands. Mom goes white, pastes on a smile, and pulls away.

"And look at you," she says, her voice breaks. "How are you feeling? Baby Boy Boyle will be here in no time."

Jenny rubs her stomach and beams.

Mom stares at her bloody hands and gags. "Would you mind if I used the ladies' room?"

Uncle Landis jumps off the tractor and spatters Lani with mud. "No problem. Septic is down, so you'll have to use the back-up."

"Back-up?" Mom looks around.

Landis points. "Outhouse. Follow that trail a piece and you'll see 'er. Should be a roll of paper on the .22."

"We'll all wait inside, Elaina." Jenny glances from me to Lani. "Except for your two beautiful kids. A wonderful mucky day like this? I'm sure you two want to get dirty." She smiles at me. "We'll call you for lunch and you can get washed up for the graveyard." ·

"Actually," I say, "I wouldn't mind — "

"Exploring with Lani." Dad raises his eyebrows.

"Well, yeah. Right. Exploring with Lani." I exhale hard, nod to Lani, who's still busy flecking dirt off her face, and we step gingerly toward the barn.

"Shoo!"

We freeze at Mom's distant scream. Footsteps slap wet ground. She reappears, gun and toilet paper in hand. Mom straightens and throws back her hair. "It is black and small and toothy."

"Oh, the mink. Landis, you didn't mention Stinker." Jenny shakes her head. "Don't know why that crazy critter made a nest beneath the outhouse, but it's harmless."

A silence descends. It's the silence of Mom's wrath. She drops the gun, her hands shoot to her hips, and she begins to puff. Bigger and bigger, like a balloon. Lani peeks at me. She knows what I know — Mom will burst and it won't be pretty.

The Barn Owl clenches her teeth, draws a screechy breath through her nose, and parts pursed lips —

"Come on in, Brother!" Landis throws his arm around Dad and they tromp toward the porch. Jenny whistles for Tripod and follows. That leaves us and Mom and a loaded gun.

I grab Lani's arm. "Time to leave."

"How long do we need to stand here?"

Lani looks at me, then back at the cow. We've been frozen by this bovine for near an hour, hands shoved deep in our pockets. Bessy hasn't moved. We won't either.

"Until the lunch bell. Seems like a safe, clean place, right?" I peek at Lani. "Unless you *want* to explore."

Lani shakes her head. "You're a loser. Don't take that personally or anything, but this place freaks you out and you know it." Lani wanders away, calls back over her shoulder. "Now that crazy Julia? If half of what kids say is true, she'd love it here." She snickers. "Wouldn't she?"

A distant cowbell clangs, and Lani races toward the house.

"My Julia." I rub my face with my hands, think about the new layer of farm bacteria covering my cheeks, and wince. "Yeah, she would."

Twenty minutes and two scrub downs later, we sit down to deer hunks and turkey slabs.

"Yes, sir." Landis gives Jenny's shoulders a gentle squeeze. "My honey sets quite a spread, does she not? A little thankfulness is in order."

Landis squeezes his eyelids tight. "Oh Lord, I am thankful for this family. I am also thankful for this meat. At this moment, I do not know which one I am more thankful for. Family or meat. I must tell the truth. But my Jenny. Where would I be without my honey? Amen."

Dad digs in. Mom pushes extra-rare meat around her plate with her pitchfork-size utensil. It leaves a blood trail.

Landis stuffs a bite into his mouth, waves his fork toward Lani and me. "Let me tell you about this buck you're eating."

Lani pauses mid-chew and lifts her napkin to her mouth.

"Last fall a deer — no, badly put — my *friend* strolls right up to the house. You'll soon understand my kinship with the animal. This was the largest ten-point buck I've ever seen. He gazes at me through that window." Landis points over his shoulder. "I say, 'Honey, bring the rifle.' She says, 'Which one,' and I say, 'I do not care; bring me a gun.' When she does, that deer cocks his head and presses his nose against the glass. Like a lost puppy. He wants to be friends. Big, gentle eyes. Beautiful animal. Lonely animal."

Lani, now a pleasant shade of green, stares straight ahead.

"And I rise. I walk outside and around the house. Wouldn't you know, that deer lets me approach to a distance of six feet? He trusts me. Completely. Would you believe that we were communing? It's not a stretch. I named him Martin, after our dearly departed older brother." Landis glances at Dad, sniffs, and grabs Jenny's hand. "I shared special moments with that deer. Marty passed so quickly. There were things I needed to say, things deep from the heart I never could say, not until that sacred animal arrived and I poured out my heart. Thirteen years of bottled-up emotion spilled out and I wept. It's true. That beautiful creature lay down and listened to me weep." Landis wipes his eyes with the heel of his hand. "I've rarely felt so close to anything in my life as that deer. 'Bless you,' I whispered. 'Bless you, Martin.' Then POW! I blasted him between the eyes!"

Mom jumps up, Lani spews Martin all over the table, and my stomach heaves. I look down at my leftover hunk of Martin. I can't do it.

"Well, that's the story of the venison. Want to hear about that turkey?"

"No," I swallow hard. "Please, no. Maybe later."

"Shoot, I understand. You're in a hurry to get to the

graveyard." Landis pushes back and stands. "Sweetie, these kids are biting to get moving. What say we leave dessert and dishes and head out?"

"Sounds wonderful, except with roads so wet — "

"Yes. We'll all be taking four-wheelers. Brother? Elaina? Children? Onward."

CHAPTER 5

"Y EEHAW!"

Uncle Landis's holler floats down from the top of a distant hill. I can't see him, but I know what he's doing. Riding rings around the hilltop cemetery. Landis loves to "war whoop" in his maniacal pre-service tribal dance.

"Fool." Mom shifts in front of me on our ATV. "One day, Martin, Uncle Landis will spin out, and we will arrive just in time to plant *him* among his forefathers. Won't that be convenient? Yeehaw, indeed!"

I hear Dad laugh too. He never laughs. Except on this day. His laughs and shouts fill the spaces between the drone of four-wheeler engines. Both Dad and his brother sound like kids. Big kids on sugar highs.

"Use some speed, Jenny." It's Landis again. "Give my son a real ride!"

Aunt Jenny squeals. Lani shrieks. She hadn't looked too healthy mounting the back of Jenny's Polaris.

I close my eyes and picture the scene. A muddy race on a bumpy track around a bunch of dead spectators. Uncle Landis in first, Dad a close second, and the team of pregnant woman, tummy boy, and whiny girl pulling up the rear.

The four-wheelers' engines snarl and rev, faster and faster.

Down in the valley, I sigh, relieved we aren't moving fast.

Of course, going Mom-slow might be worse.

"Hold tight to the disaster pack, Martin." Mom accelerates to three miles per hour. "A fall could mean an instant and gruesome end."

"Instant *and* gruesome?"

"Are you obsessing about death again? You must let that go and enjoy your childhood."

"But you brought up — "

"Watch out!"

I reach around her backpack and get a vice grip on Mom's waist. She slaps my hands.

"Let me breathe or I'll lose control completely."

Already happened.

I loosen my grasp and follow Mom's gaze, all the way down to the washed-out trail that leads straight up cemetery hill. A squirrel leaps playfully around our ATV.

Mom peeks over her shoulder. "See what I mean? In the wilderness, even gentle creatures attack with reckless abandon."

The animal seems harmless. "We're being attacked?"

"Predators typically toy with their prey before they plunge their teeth into unsuspecting flesh." She nods. "Do not be fooled. There is white on the face. Foam, no doubt. You know what that means. R-A-B-I-E-S."

Some words are simply too horrible for her to say. She squeezes the brake. "Do not move," she whispers.

We sit motionless. A mosquito buzzes my ear, lands on my neck, and begins to drink. I want to whack it, but Mom's being vigilant and I don't dare move. The bug finishes her transfusion, pumps me full of itch juice, and flies away. I wince and glare at our stalker.

"I think that foam is a whitish A-C-O-R-N."

"Drop the attitude, Martin, and marvel at the cleverness of this creature. It used a decoy in the attack."

Yes, they are very clever, and I hold my breath. The sneaky beast bounds off, I scratch my neck with gusto, and Mom inches our ATV forward. Minutes pass, and I check the speedometer.

I cup my hand around Mom's ear. "Are you sure we're moving?"

"Yes." She straightens and gives the accelerator a flutter. We crunch ahead. "The others may have reached the cemetery first, but we will reach it alive — mud!"

I jerk back and peek around Mom. Our front wheels lodge in a muddy pool and our tires spin, sludge-caked and helpless.

"Maybe if we used more speed?" I say.

"Twice stuck," Mom mutters. "Twice stuck, raw meat, jeopardizing the children."

Venting has begun. We will be here for a while. I stare around. Oak and elm lock knobby arms and form a green ceiling that presses down on me. All around, the woods poke gnarled fingers toward my head. They creak and rustle and want to grab me. I'm quickly claustrophobic.

"I'm going to walk the rest of the way, is that okay with you?"

"Abnormally large rodents beneath the outhouse, toilet paper on loaded guns ..."

Mom's a lister, and right now she can't hear me. She's only listed five horrors and I know she won't run out of problems until she hits thirty, so I slip off the back of the ATV and watch my sneakers disappear in the mud. I lift a foot. No shoe.

"Mud ate my Adidas!"

I close my eyes, reach my hand into the muck, and feel leather. I strain and tug and slowly the ground releases my shoe with a slurp. I step off the trail, scrape out the mud, and jam in my foot. And walk.

"They're only trees. They're only ugly trees. They're only, boy-hating ugly trees. They're only boy-hating, ugly, hungry — "

A branch grabs my arm. I break into a run.

The higher I stumble, the wider the trail gets until it spreads out into a field covered with daisies and tread marks. My heartbeat slows and I bend at the waist, searching for air.

I peek down at the path. Far below Mom sits cross-armed on the stuck four-wheeler. In front of me, surrounded by tombstones, the others gather in a circle: The Circle of Death.

The ceremony is about to begin.

They stand in silence except for Lani, who moans and clutches her stomach.

"Martin, my boy!" Landis breaks from the group and approaches, smiling at my legs and feet. "I wouldn't have imagined that you two would go muddin'."

"First time for everything." I force a weak smile. "We got stuck. She's still down there."

He peers over my shoulder.

"Hmm. She wasn't tickled about the ride up."

"No," I say. "We were attacked."

"Bear?"

"Rabid squirrel."

"Brother! Your wife needs you."

Dad jogs toward us and stops at my side. He stares down the hill, his eyes soft. He slaps Landis on the back and shoots me a wink. "Looks like my wife needs a hero. Step aside, gentlemen."

I watch Dad traipse down through the muck.

"C'mon, Martin." Landis rounds my shoulder with his arm. "Sometimes a man's best intentions lead to words. Best let 'em spill out in private."

Soon we've all passed beneath the wrought iron arch that marks the Boyle Family graveyard. I look at Lani. She's green again. Mom's a deep shade of crimson. Landis and Dad are muddy brown. I'm pale — I can feel it.

Dad slips a small journal from his pocket and steps into the center of our circle. He holds his breath. I hold mine.

To my right, Landis whispers, "Don't hold back, now. Preach it, Brother."

"Look around you, Boyles." Dad waves about with his free hand. "What do you see?"

Lani leans over and gasps, "Rotting bones?"

"Heroism. Courage. The men in this field died fighting for their families, their country, their very survival." Dad's voice strengthens. He's in his glory, and he gestures big and spins fast. "This field is a history book filled with stories. Our family's stories. Stories of adventure and danger and the putrid stench of war."

"Hear, hear!" Landis pumps his fist in the air. Jenny kicks him in the shin and he slowly lowers his arm. "Sorry, Gav. I got carried away there. Go on, now."

"Pouring from the veins of my dear oldest brother Marty, and spilling forth from every other Martin including the first, infantryman Martin Boyle, born in 1790, the blood in this ground on which you stand cries out. Listen! Can you hear? Yes, this mud oozes with Boyle blood — "

Lani heaves deer chunks. They splat over my muddy shoes.

Uncle Landis leans forward, nods, and pounds his chest. "The truth hits you down deep, don't it girl?"

Mom extracts a towel from the disaster pack, wipes Lani's face, and shoots Dad her icicle look. But Dad's gaze is occupied. He faces me with gleaming eyes. He bends and grabs a fistful of mud. Then he straightens, raises that paw before his face, and lets brown smear seep out the cracks between his fingers. "Yes, Boyle blood. It's a special time when we can honor the fallen. Especially for *you*."

"Me?" I ask.

"You." His gaze won't let mine go.

My fingertips prickle.

"As the firstborn in our family, you inherited a name full of meaning and history. Martin." He gestures toward a small stone. "The life of the first Martin was so filled with courage, men said there could only be one Martin."

Inside, my stomach turns and I close my eyes. When

I open them, the world is fuzzy and my head is light. I touch my forehead. It burns. I'm a Martin furnace and I think I might die on the spot.

"Clawing through a frozen wasteland ..." Dad scratches at the air. "Freshly killed turkey and rabbit strapped to his back, Martin provided food for a fort's hacking, bleeding, weeping inhabitants."

"Dang, that's good." Landis sniffs.

"Air," I whisper. "I need some air."

Mom walks over and places the back of her hand against my brow. "Now both children have fallen ill." She turns and thumps Lani's back. My sister hurls again. Mom must be too hot to notice. "This ceremony must end before someone gets hurt!"

"Hey, brother, go back to the Boyle blood section. That part done grows goosebumps on my hide." Landis gets another kick from his wife, and he scowls. "Well, it does."

Jenny sighs, and then frowns at Lani. "She's likely not used to consuming wild game. It's an acquired taste. Why don't we take a chicken when we get back? Ever whacked the head off a chicken, Lani?"

Lani covers her mouth and shakes her head.

"To continue." Dad raises his hand and clears his throat. "Our history is filled with sacrifice." His voice rises. "Allow me now to expand on a few such stories."

Please, Dad, no expanding!

I blink hard and step back out of the circle. Nobody notices the absence of Fever Boy, and soon Dad's voice garbles in the distance. He doesn't seem to notice that I've vanished. Mom screeches and Jenny scolds and everyone speaks at once. I turn from my family and stagger among the stones, where my footing steadies and my head cools.

A wind gust fills my nose with after-rain smell and whisks away the droplets clinging to the field's tall grass. Hemmed in by thick woods, the graveyard rests on the edge of Uncle Landis's land. It looks nothing like an In Between graveyard. There's nothing neat or manicured about it. Headstones are spaced unevenly, and most poke out of the ground at weird angles, like maybe the dead guy underneath is pushing real hard to escape.

I reach the back row of stones, inhale hard, and read:

Martin Boyle. Martin Boyle. Martin Boyle.

"Too many dead Martins, if you ask me." I bite my lip hard.

I check the family. The Barn Owl still hoots.

Guess there's no need to hurry.

I kneel in front of the smallest headstone. "So you're the first Martin. What was your mom like?"

The crumbling stone doesn't answer. I squint at the etching. Only the letters *MART* remain, along with mossy scratching beneath.

"Landis isn't taking care of you very well." I reach for a stick and scrape at greenish fuzz. Minutes later, the date comes clear.

"1790 – 1820. You are way old! Even for a dead guy."

My knees stiffen and I shuffle next door to a big old stone, cocked to the left and cracked in half.

MARTIN BOYLE

The birth date is missing, but his death year is as clear as Mom's dinner bell — *1835*. I peek at the next marker.

"Wait a minute," I whisper, stand, and step back. "You *died* in 1835." I point at the next one. "And you ..." I scamper down the row. "You were *born* in 1835."

My eyes widen and my legs wobble as I quick-step down the row of moldy Martins. "1835–1865. 1865–1899. 1899–1956. 1956–1998."

I push both hands through matted hair. Sweat drops sting my eyes.

One dies, one is born. There's always a Martin. There's only one Martin.

I plop into the mud in front of my dad's older brother. He died so fast. He died so ... 1998.

"The year I was born." I stare at the hideous pattern on the stones. "When a new Martin is born, the living one dies." My mind races.

My name is cursed!

"Think, think. Any other Martins in the family?" I breathe deeply. "Just me. I'm fine. I'm the only living Martin." I lean back and chuckle, then laugh.

That was close. That was really close.

"Get out of that mud, Martin. Do you have any idea how many germs hide in a place like this?" I look back at the ceremony. Mom's hands shoot to her hips. "Antibac. Now."

I stand, a smeary butt for the second time today, and search my pocket for hand sanitizer. It's a happy search. I've been given a second chance at life.

"'Course you know, Lani, that soon as you hack off the hen's head, she'll start twitchin' and floppin.' In fact, the last one fluttered a minute against my chest. Talk about bloody suspenders. That'll startle the tar right out of you."

"Stop scaring the girl, Landis!" Aunt Jenny fumes. She'd probably kick him with both feet if she could. But then she'd fall and that would be bad for the little one —

My gaze zooms in on her gut, and I drop my bottle of scrub. The little one.

Aunt Jenny carries the first child in their family. It's a boy. They will name him Martin after the Boyle tradition.

There can only be one Martin.

I stare at the row of headstones, at the space next to Dad's brother. My space.

Lani vomits again, but this time I don't care.

When that kid is born ...

"I'm going to die."

CHAPTER 6

I WONDER WHAT DYING FEELS LIKE.

The question has haunted me since the cemetery. On our silent drive back from Landis's. Throughout a sleepless night. It sticks with me now.

I walk the rails westward; my house long vanished behind me. I've never been this far down the tracks at 5:30 in the morning without the Barn Owl's permission. I shiver and clutch the whistle that hangs around my neck. One tweet on the safety device would activate Mom's bowels and bring her screeching to my side.

"Death. The last gasp. The big send off. Dust to dust. Farewell, cruel world." I pry a stake from the track and point it at the sky. "It's not fair. Being dead isn't fair," I whisper. "How was Disneyland, Martin? Sorry, never been there. Do you have your driver's license? No, corpses can't parallel park."

My free hand cups around my mouth, and I whip

the stake toward the clouds. "I mean, what did I do to you? What did I do to anybody? Sure, I put a little hot sauce in Lani's eyedrops, and I did cover her toilet with Saran Wrap, but those don't deserve —"

The stake plummets to earth and impales the dirt between my feet.

Cripes! What do you have against Martins?

I break into a run, a stumbling, angry run that carries me away from the tracks and toward the outfield wall of Midway Stadium.

The field looms large and foreboding and empty. I clank into the ten-foot security fence down the right field line and tug at the loose chains connecting oversized gates. I release the chain links and glance at my hands, covered with rust.

Note to self. Check on tetanus booster.

I hold my breath, think skinny thoughts, and squeeze between the gates and into the stadium. I straighten on the right-field warning track and inspect my arms for scratches and skin breaks.

Minutes later I plunk down on the bleachers, surrounded by ten thousand empty seats.

Nobody will miss me anyway.

I stare at the field, groomed and waiting — waiting for a living kid to leave cleat marks on the base paths. How great would it have been to play baseball, run track — anything?

"Next up ... Martin Boyle! They're carrying him out right now. He's looking a little stiff. What's that? Duct tape? Yes, sports fans, his teammates are yanking him out of the coffin and duct-taping a bat to his hands! Have you ever seen anything — "

"Popcorn! Peanuts!"

I jump and reach for the whistle around my neck.

"Kinda early for you, isn't it, Marty?" Grimy waves from the upper deck and slowly makes his way down the aisle. "Your mom'll blow when she finds you gone."

Poole doesn't look so scary. Not now. He strolls by me onto the top of the dugout, where he plops down and dangles his feet. Not a grimy care in the world.

"I'm thankful for this beautiful morning!" He points toward the sky. "See that sunrise? Smell that air — "

"That's stink from the rendering plant."

"Someone's having a bad day." He grins. "Shame too. Such a glorious — "

"Stop it! You don't have ... issues. Well, maybe an ongoing odor problem, but besides that, no issues. I, on the other hand, might look normal — "

"You don't."

"Whatever. I look normaller than you." I hold up a hand and rub my knuckles. "But you, at least, might live to get arthritis."

Poole frowns. "And that's a good thing?"

I leap to my feet, pause, and kick the bleacher in

front of me. "You have no idea what's going on — okay, that hurt my toe — where was I?"

"Um. You have no idea — "

"Right," I say. "You go where you want and sleep where you want and take a shower every third week — "

"Fourth."

"... fourth week. And you have a whole grimy life in front of you. Seventy, eighty, ninety grimy years."

I breathe hard. I've never yelled at anyone like that before. Poole yawns at me, like he's waiting for more, but I'm exhausted. "Sorry, yesterday was tough and today is tougher and tomorrow ..."

"Tomorrow?" He stands.

I drop my gaze. "I found out I don't have too many of them."

Poole exhales, long and slow. "You don't look sick."

"Not sick." I bury my face in my hands and feel the wet. "Cursed. See, Dad named me Martin."

"Tragic." He wears a thinking face. "A Martin Boyle curse. What are ya going to do?"

He's an idiot. Die! I'm going to die!

"You don't believe me."

"Didn't say that. It's just not something you see much in obituaries." Poole lifts his hand and traces an invisible headline. *"Boy Killed by His Name."* He stretches. "Are you into baseball?"

"I'm telling you I'm curse — I, uh, think I'd love

baseball. Mom never let me play. Dirt fungi. It grows around the base paths, then gets beneath the fingernails and causes cuticle rot — "

"Follow me." Poole leaps off the top of the dugout and disappears from view. I scamper forward and peer over the edge. Grimy stands on the spongy field near the batter's box. He waves me down. "Jump, Martin."

I shake my head. "Five foot rule. Did you know that if you freefall more than five feet you have a better than thirty percent chance of doing internal damage to the ligaments near your ankle?"

Poole glares with that Dad glare. It pulls me forward. I sit down, grab my whistle, and slip off. I land hard and my ankles scream.

"My feet! Oh, oh, here comes the ache ... Yow! I told you — "

"You're fine. Shake 'em out and wait here." Poole vanishes into a small stadium door and quickly reappears.

"Okay, slugger, you're in luck. I know Frank, the watchman. He lets me use the equipment. Here you go." Poole tosses a bat toward home plate and shoves a pitching machine toward the mound.

He whistles. A vagrant shouldn't be whistling. I frown. "You really live in my backyard."

"No. Your house is in my front yard, but it's all in how you see it." Poole sets down a bucket filled with baseballs.

"And you sleep out there," I say.

"Yep."

"Don't you get cold?"

"Yep."

"Hungry? Where do you get food?"

Poole turns the pitching machine toward home plate and leans over the top. "Those tomatoes you paint are always mighty tasty. Now, that pumpkin years back was certainly a letdown."

I frown, and Poole rolls his eyes. "Frank checks in on me now and then." He raises a hand. "Any more questions?"

I adjust my glasses. "Not right now."

"Good." He straightens. "Here's how this works. You stand at the plate, I'll load 'er up and fire you some balls. Plaster 'em!"

"But I don't know how to — "

"Exactly, and it sounds like you don't have much time." He grins. "Now or never."

I bend over and pick up the bat, turn it around in my hands. "This curse is *not* my imagination."

Poole slips twenty balls into a duffel and slings the bag over his shoulder. "Doesn't matter what I think. Besides, you don't live much anyway." He points at the batter's box. "Play ball!"

I inch closer, place the bat on my shoulder. "Those aren't going to come fast, are they?"

Whoosh. Inches from my nose. I fall to the ground, jump up quick, and swipe dirt off my shirt. Fungi everywhere. "That's slow?"

"Fire!" he hoots.

Whoosh! The ball skims my rear.

"How do ya like that one?" Poole pumps his fist into the air.

"What are you do — "

"Run. Martin, run!" He fires another ball, pegs my calf.

"Ah!"

"Direct hit!" Poole leaps and dances and shoves the machine toward me. "Run!"

My eyes widen, and I take off for first.

Zing!

Poole falls in behind and chases me to first. "Faster!"

"You're crazy!" I jam my whistle in my mouth and start tweeting.

Zoom!

"Oh!" Tweet! "That hit my back." Tweet, tweet. I speed to second.

Poole chases me three times around the bases before I collapse in the fungi jungle near home plate. "Fine," I gasp. "Finish me off. It'll happen soon anyway."

Poole nudges me with his foot. "So what are you going to do now?"

I groan. "Ice my butt."

"Sorry 'bout that. Didn't see any other way to get you to play." He kneels. "So you'll go home and what, sit in the tub? Plan your funeral?"

"You think this is funny." I push to all fours, wince, and slowly stand.

He shakes his head. "Like I said, what I think doesn't matter much, does it?"

I shuffle away from Poole and into the outfield. It's a long walk home, and there's a barn owl in a panic by now.

"Good heavens, Martin!" Mom throws open the door and pulls me in by the arm. "Where have you been?" She squints at my neck, grabs my collar, yanks, and peeks at my back. "Bruises. Everywhere. Who did this to you?"

"A kid." I step toward the stairs, but her grasp stiffens.

"A ruffian, no doubt. We need to document the damage or the police won't take this seriously."

"Police?"

Her hands shoot to her hips. "Martin, you're a victim of A-S-S-A-U-L-T. This is a police matter. Strip!"

"What?" I glance around the living room. "Here? Now?"

Lani bounds down the stairs. She looks at me and grimaces. "Who beat you up?"

I roll my eyes. "A kid."

Her eyes are huge, like I did something great. "Cool! Did you fight him off?"

"Not exactly."

"Strip to your boxers, Martin." Mom fiddles with her digital camera.

I point at Lani. "Not in front of — "

"Oh, for Pete's sake, you used to share a tub. This is nothing new."

"Ew!" Lani dashes up the stairs, and I move into the kitchen.

I wince and pull my shirt off. Mom gasps and reaches for the camera. "My son, my son. What has this ruffian done to you?" Click. "The pain." Click. "A mother should never have to see this kind of — turn around, Martin — injury inflicted on her child." Click.

She captures my spots of black, blue, and yellow from all angles. "Now the police cannot shirk their responsibilities. They'll find your assailant and throw him behind bars. And you can believe that at his trial we will have words. Oh yes, we will have word — "

"But I know my assailant." I grimace into my shirt and limp from the room. "We were just playing baseball. I fell. Sort of. A lot."

"Who was it? Who? Who?" cries the Barn Owl.

Monday morning comes quickly and painfully.

I gimp to the mirror. A particularly nasty neck bruise mocks me, and I gingerly push a comb through my hair.

"School. Neck bruise. Bad combination." I stroke my blue skin with my fingers. "Make-up? No. Face paint? No ..."

Turtleneck!

I pick the weighty red one, the Christmas one with the battery sewn inside. Touch near my heart and Christmas trees will flash to the musical stylings of chipmunks singing *pa-rum-pa-pum-pum*. But at least it's way big and hides the bottom of my chin.

Perspiration gathers and beads. It drips near the brow, at the neck, in the pits. The shirt is muggy and a scorcher but this woolen tomb is my only choice. I haul sore muscles down the steps and stop.

8 x 11 portraits hang all around the living room. Post-it notes title each picture.

Martin Boyle's abdomen.

Martin Boyle's left thigh.

I walk into the kitchen. Six magnets clip a life-sized blow-up of my mottled rear to the fridge.

"Officer Wilkins will be stopping by around ten."

Mom pours coffee at the table. "He describes the incident as petty, but these pictures will change his mind." She sips and gestures toward my buttocks with her mug. "I affixed Post-it arrows to highlight the most painful blows."

I shake my head and trudge out of the kitchen just as Lani rushes in. "There better be a bagel — Gross! There's a photo of Martin's butt on the fridge. How am I supposed to eat?"

I slip out of the house, find a nice-sized stone, and kick it all the way to the bus stop. The sun burns, too hot for April, and by the time I arrive I'm a nappy-haired, bruise-butted sweatball.

"Dressed a little warm, aren't cha?" Charley runs toward me, pencil and paper in hand.

"I was out of clean shorts and T-shirts." I yank at my collar. "It doesn't matter any — "

"Big favor time." Charley shoves the paper into my chest. "I really need some more of that knight story." He starts to dance. The Charley Dance. His arms, legs, and hips all gyrate at the same time. Frightening. "And put in plenty of love-o-rama between the knight and what's her name."

"Alia."

"Yeah, her. Lots of love stuff. And I need it before third hour or I'm going to look dumb."

I shrug. "You do look dumb."

The bus's brakes squeal. We clamor in and take our seats.

"No air bag?" Charley backhands my chest. "What's the deal?"

I think on that. "Just forgot. I forgot the mask too. And the sanitizer and my vitamin C tablets. I forgot everything." I pause and sneak a peek at my friend. "Say, Charley, I, uh, found out something at the cemetery."

"Your mom is bizarre and your dad's stuck in the 1800s."

How do I tell my best friend I'll be dead in three months?

I stare straight ahead and breathe deeply. "Three more months is all I got."

"It's so great!" His beady eyes sparkle. "Can't wait for summer myself. But about the story. You know, *The White Knight*? I gave you some more time to think about it." He holds a pencil beneath my nose. "What are you going to do now?"

I shoot Charley a glance. "What am I going to do now? You're the second person in two days who's asked me — Where did you hear that?"

"Hear what?"

The bus bounces over the repaired pothole and my friend babbles on, but I don't listen. *What am I going to do now? I have three months.*

I sit up straight. *Three months.*

I peek at Charley. He's still talking.

"… see, so I know you probably didn't want to hear that, but it's really going great between me and Julia …"

Julia.

CHAPTER 7

FIRST PERIOD PHYS ED. FIFTY MINUTES OF EMBAR-rassment. I sit sweaty-necked in the locker room watching other boys suit up.

Mr. Halden lumbers in. "Get dressed, Boyle," he booms. "Then march that underdeveloped body of yours into the weight room." Halden checks his watch. "You're two minutes from late. You know what that means, boy." He cracks a hideous smile and then his knuckles. "You're asking for The Treatment."

The Treatment. Sweating turns to shivering. I've never gotten The Treatment. Nobody has. Halden's sinister threat is so terrifying, we all hop to. But today I can't hop, not in my chipmunk turtleneck. Halden leaves and I stare into my open locker at my perfect blue T-shirt and perfect blue shorts and wonder what's coming.

Will runs into the locker room, laughs, and points at the clock. "You're not going to make it! Halden's in his office preparing your Treatment. Move, you idiot."

Suddenly the room fills with boys. The chant begins. "Treatment! Treatment!"

From the back room, Halden hollers. "Here it comes. First time in thirty years I've ever had to administer this. Boyle? Office. Now."

I nod and push to my feet. "I'm coming, I'm coming." Head drooped, I shuffle between jeering lines of frothy boys ... and dash for the locker room door.

"Catch him!" Will hollers and dives for my feet. I stumble but stay vertical and explode into the hall, serenaded by helium-lunged chipmunks.

"Get 'em, boys!" Halden releases his demented herd. It's the running of the bulls, and I'm wearing red, and if I slip, I'm toast. I fishtail around the corner.

... pa-pum-pum. "Shush, sweater."

Girls' bathroom!

Panic pushes me inside. I leap into a stall, slam the door, and hop on the bowl. My heartbeat steadies, my head thuds against the door, and I swallow hard.

This is crazy!

Hinges creak and I brace myself, peeking out the crack.

Oh no.

"Crazy guys," Keira says. "Wonder what Martin did."

"Probably squirted someone with Germ-X." My Julia tosses her hair back and peers into the mirror.

I don't have my Germ-X today, thank you very much!

"Whatever it is, I feel sorry for the guy, you know?" Keira turns and leans against the sink. "He seems nice."

"How would you know? He's mute. And he's been in my classes since, like, kindergarten. I don't think he has a tongue. But whatever, Charley's different." Julia glances down. "I almost told him about my parents yesterday. He's so easy to talk to."

"And dumb."

"That's what I thought." Julia smiles and bites her lip. "And then he wrote this story, well a piece of a story, and ... it's so, I don't know, like romantic or something. Everything's different. Does that make any sense?"

"You like Charley because of a story?"

My story!

"He's supposed to bring the next part today, third hour."

Keira pulls Julia toward the door. "You're crazy."

"Maybe, but —"

Yipping voices of frothy gym boys echo in the hall.

"Hey, Julia, have you seen Martin?" Will shouts.

"What do you think? I've been in a bath —"

Slam. The bathroom is very quiet. I let my head fall against the stall door with a thud.

Pa-rum-pa-pum-pum! I grab at my turtleneck. "Stupid chipmunks."

I close my eyes. "See, Julia? I do have a tongue."

I pass the time in the bathroom, which makes me late to every class. Flimsy tardy slips are better than the attacks of rabid gym boys.

But there's no escaping the pack during lunch hour.

I race to the round table, the one tucked in the lunchroom corner. *Stay low, eat fast, and pray. Stay low, eat fast, and* — Charley.

My best friend drapes over the isolation table. I ease up behind him.

"Charley?" I peek over my shoulder. "You dead?"

"Wish I was. I'm such a loser." He lets out a moan.

I plop down. "I won't argue with that."

Charley lifts his head and squints. "It's mostly *your* fault. A true friend would've given me a page, a paragraph, anything to make Julia happy, but no! You had to hold back. And after all we've been through."

I want to feel bad for my friend, but I can't. "So what — "

"I'll tell you what! I wrote the next section of the

story and …" His forehead thuds against the table. "I showed Julia."

"*You* added to my story?" I clear my throat. "Couldn't have been that bad."

Charley digs in his back pocket, pulls out a ratty sheet of notebook paper, and slaps it down in front of me. I smooth the paper and read.

The night was scared. The night was angry. The other night was scared and angry. They were scared and angry at each other. They hit each other. The white night hit the black night. The black night hit the white night. They both said ouch.

"Oh boy," I whisper.

"She had these beautiful drawings. She spent days working on them." Charley buries his head in his hands, then spreads his fingers to talk through the cracks. "She said she couldn't get the story out of her mind and then — they both said 'ouch'? What was I thinking?"

I exhale hard. "You know, maybe I should have — "

"There he is!"

I glance around me. A ring of boys encircles the table. "Halden's looking for you."

"He'll probably forget, right?" I say. "He has other kids to torture."

"Next time we have gym …" Will slaps my back. "I wouldn't want to be you."

He scans the lunchroom and grins. "Hey, Halden's in the teachers' line. Over here, Mr. Halden!"

The pack snickers, and I jump. "Gotta go, Charley."

I push through the circle, duck behind lines of tray-shuttling kids, and slither into the hall.

Where to hide. Where to hide. Media Center!

I take a sharp left, scamper through the hall, and turn right at the book showcase. I burst in the door and Ms. Kellian sets down an armful of heavy books. "Hello, Martin. It's been a while."

"Tough couple days." I breathe heavily and pat a computer screen. "Can I hide behind one of these?"

"Be my guest."

I sit and twiddle on the keyboard. The Treatment and Julia and my lunchroom escape fill my mind, but now in the silence, a cloud descends. I hate being chased, but at least I'm moving. In three months, nobody will chase me. They'll look down at me; I'll stare without blinking — face up, from a box. I can see it now ...

"Come on, Mr. Halden." Will yanks on his sleeve. "Can't you give him The Treatment?"

The funeral home erupts. "Treatment! Treatment!"

"Hush, boys. No, we can't. Look at him. Dead as a doorknob." Mr. Halden leans over my stiff body and whispers, "You got off easy, kid."

I blink hard and my arms feel heavy. I've been angry since the cemetery. But not now. My body slumps and my eyes sting.

I want to cry.

"Cruel. Fool. Gruel. Poole," I mutter, and mindlessly whack the keyboard. "How come all rotten words rhyme? Hearse. Worse. Curse . . ."

I Google *geneology* and enter my name and city. "There I am. Let's find the other unfortunates. *Martin Boyle*. Enter." The screen fills with former Martins' birth and death dates, the pattern undeniable. I click on the first Martin link.

Died heroically at Fort Snelling.

How can everyone miss these dates? Dad should know the curse's pattern.

I straighten, click *print*, and grab the sheet off the tray. There's no way out. It's time to tell the family of my impending doom, starting with the one who matters most.

I run home from the bus stop, salty sweat coating my lips. I have sixty minutes of unhindered Dad time. Then the Owl alights and lunacy begins.

I leap up the steps, stumble through the door. "Dad? Dad!"

Footsteps shuffle above me. I pound up the stairs. "Are you up here?"

"Higher!"

Not the attic.

My room rests on the only secure level of our home. The Owl's nest and Underwear World lie beneath my feet. The creaky, microbial, spore-filled attic promises danger overhead. I live between, sandwiched safe and sanitary, and more than once have vowed never to climb the stairs at the hall's end.

"Come up here and help me!" Dad calls.

I clutch the paper that proves the curse and tiptoe toward the steps. Above me, the attic floor creaks and pops. Unfinished attic hardwood turns every step Dad takes into a scene from a horror flick.

I reach the stairway and think of Poole.

Creak. Pop.

Whistle a happy tune. Think, Marty. Anything cheery and —

Creak.

There are no happy tunes in my world. Life is like the door at the top of the steps — closed and dark and —

That door flies open and Dad smiles. "Come on up, I want to show you something."

I climb into a cobweb-infested attic. It smells of must and mothballs.

"Here." Dad whispers, and bends over in the corner.

I walk, slow and silent as a cat, to where he stoops. He glances at me, winks, and pulls back a swath of insulation. "Ever seen a sleeping bat?"

Fuzzy, black-winged mice clump in a heap on the floorboards. I jerk back and my head slams against a ceiling beam. I stagger limp-legged toward the door.

"They've been sleeping here?" I wince and massage my skull. "Right above my head?"

"Your mother doesn't know. She'd be none too pleased." Dad reaches out and strokes a beast. "There, there. Cute little fella. Want to pet one?"

I jam my hands deep into my pockets.

Dad nods. "They're fast asleep. I'll need to remove them, but don't you think they give the house character?"

"Remove them?"

Dad points over my shoulder to the far wall. Sheets of contact paper, coated with dismembered bat heads and wings, cover the rafters. Bat bodies ball on the floor beneath.

"The little guys get stuck and pull and pull. They yank so hard their heads pop off."

A rumbling begins deep in my stomach. I can feel the burn in my throat. I'm five seconds from sick.

Death everywhere. I run down the steps, race the length of the hall, and duck into the bathroom. I sit on the side of the tub and prepare for a violent stomach lurch. Dad's steady footsteps approach.

"I didn't mean to frighten you, son." He steps inside the bathroom, sweeps away the shower curtain, and eases down beside me. "I thought you might be interested to see who lives here besides us."

"Yeah, well." I swallow and lift the pulpy paper to his nose. "There will be one less here soon."

Dad uncrumples the sheet and studies it top to bottom. His gaze shifts to me. "I'm going to ask you a serious question, Martin. I need you to be truthful. How long have you been thinking about death?"

"A little while."

He puffs out a blast of air. "I know I'm not around much, but it looks like I need to be. Would you consider talking to a counselor?"

"About …"

"This obsession with dying." He makes a fist and bumps my thigh. "Your mother mentioned it after our cemetery visit. I thought she was being her quirky self but maybe — "

I grab the sheet back. "I am not the problem. Look!" I point at the dates. "Don't you see a pattern here? And in three short months, who is going to be born? Uncle Landis's Martin Boyle. And who is going to die?" I point at myself. "Your Martin Boyle. This is not an obsession. Does this not look a bit curse-like to you?"

He shifts into thinking gear.

"Please, Dad. Say something."

"You think you'll die in a few months? My counselor friend specializes in helping veterans following their tours of duty. He's an expert on death fixations. He can help."

"I don't need a shrink." I lift the page. "I need anti-curse lotion or un-naming powder or something! Dad ..." I lower my voice. "I need ... I need help."

He puts his arm around me. It's been awhile since he's done that and it feels so good. I bury my head in his big shoulder. Everything will be okay.

"I see. Yes, Martin. You need help. And that's what Dr. Stanker can give you."

"You don't believe me." I push away from Dad, fly down the stairs, and into the backyard. "The man is blind." I stare at the numbers on the sheet. "What is hard to see about this?"

"What, friend?"

Poole yawns and stretches and leans against the garden train.

I throw the page at him; it bounces off his chest. Poole bends over, flattens the sheet over his thigh, and reads. Two seconds later his gaze raises to me. The paper flutters to the ground.

"You *are* going to die."

CHAPTER 8

I START A NEW ROUTINE. I CALL IT THE BIG PACE. EACH afternoon, I log hours wearing a trail in front of the boxcar.

I'm hyperaware of my body — each twinge, each sensation. Especially each wave of dizziness. They waft over me like the scent of mashed skunk. And like skunk stink, they don't blow over. The confusion sticks.

Mom stares out at me through the kitchen window. Her nose twitches, and her fingers tap nervously on her lips. I don't care. The Big Pace calms me and clears my head. There's got to be a way out of this. A back door. There must be a way to cough up death's hook and swim away from this mess.

Poole seems to enjoy my torment. Today he joins me in crisscrossing the grass. I peek at the window. No Mom. Where is the Owl when you need her?

"Let me guess," Poole says. We meet in the middle of the yard. "He thinks you're nuts."

"Excuse me?" We continue on, turn, and meet back in the middle.

"Your dad." Poole points toward the house. "The man thinks you're crazy."

"Certified."

It's been weeks since Poole pelted me. I know I'm supposed to stay far away from violent vagrants, but this one half-believes me. That changes things — if only he could keep his mouth shut.

On our next pass, he grabs my arm, and I glare.

"It's not your fault, Marty. Adults never get this stuff." He lets go. "They don't know that words have power."

"Words what?"

"Your string of dead Martins isn't a coincidence. Your name is cursed. And a curse means words. Maybe written, maybe spoken. Words have power." Poole forces his hand through his hair and exhales hard. "Why do you think I'm still here?"

"I don't know. You'll outlive me, so maybe you think you'll inherit the house."

He rolls his eyes and smirks. "Follow me. I'll show you something."

Poole hops on the track and heads east, toward the depot. I glance over my shoulder at my back door. I take three steps after him and pause. "Couldn't you describe whatever it is from here?"

Poole says nothing, and I scamper to catch up. One track turns to two, then four, and soon rails stretch in all directions. Midway Depot. BNSF. Canada. Even Amtrak. Every train in the city must pass through this bottleneck. Train cars rattle tracks beneath my feet, and I leap off the rail each time I feel vibrations.

But Poole doesn't flinch. A train rushes by on the next track over, and he doesn't flinch. Poole just smiles and waits for me, and on one occasion, points to a wrought iron bench in the middle of the yard. Poole hops over, sits, and stretches. He's in his glory.

I won't sit. Too many birds have flown overhead and left their mark on the seat.

"Your boxcar isn't my home; it's more like my summer cabin. *This* ..." Poole waves his arms around him. "... is home." He leans back, sighs, and clasps fingers behind his head.

"You don't like your family?"

Poole sighs. "Getting right to it, now, aren't we? This *is* family." He stares out at a slow-moving Burlington caboose. "There. The last place I saw my dad. Wavin' off the back end of a caboose. He drove engines all his life." He nods. "See, Ma had taken off and it was Dad and me and the trains." He pats the bench. "Take a load off. The bird stuff's dry."

I take off my T-shirt, lay it across the metal, and join him. Poole exhales hard and continues.

"Well, Ma's leaving made a mess, 'cause Dad would be gone for days at a time. But you know about that."

I nod.

He points at the depot. "When Dad was gone, the railroad guys took care of me. So that was home. Then one day —" Poole nods toward the train, now in the distance. "Dad went around that bend, and I heard a squeal, and men shouting. Dad's big ol' heart stopped and that was that. Max, the conductor, tracked down my ma, got her on the phone. First time I'd talked to her in years. She said, 'Wait right there at Midway, honey. I'm comin' back for you.'" Poole's eyes glaze, and his gaze sticks trance-like to the ground. "'I'll be back for you,'" he whispers. "Well, I'm still waitin'."

Minutes pass and I clear my throat. "How long ago —"

"Comin' on three years." He blinks and shakes his head. "See, words have power. I can't bring myself to leave. What if she comes and I'm gone?"

Poole changes before my eyes. Twenty minutes ago he was a grimy vagrant. Not now. Now, I feel for him. I don't want him in my boxcar. I want him in our guest bedroom.

"So why'd I tell you? I don't know. Ain't told anybody in so long, it felt good." He straightens, stands, and breathes deeply. "What a beautiful day."

I frown. "Okay, right there. You did that oh-everything-is-so-wonderful thing again. Your dad's dead, and your mom ... well, you always talk way happy, but you live in a boxcar, and you don't have family or Band-aids or soap or ..."

Poole dashes from the bench and leaps onto a stationary locomotive. "But I have one thing you don't. Thankfulness, my friend. My dad's medicine. He started taking it the day Mom left." Poole points. "Each day he'd come round that bend and shout out something he still had to be grateful for. Maybe he was trying to convince himself, don't know. I picked up on the habit the day he died. Helps somehow." Poole jumps off the train.

I glance at Poole's ankles and wince. "Why's it help?"

"Don't have a clue. I reckon if I feel thankful when life stinks, I must actually be thanking Someone." Poole points up. "Strange way of prayin', but it works for me. How 'bout you? Ever felt thankful, Martin? For the warm sun on your face?"

"Without sunblock?"

"Marty, Marty." He walks back to me. "Try it."

"Try—"

"Every stinkin' day, say something you're thankful for. But you got to do it out loud. You have to hear yourself say it. Words have power, you know. Here's an example for you."

He cups his hands to his mouth and yells. "Hallelujah! I'll never have to wear dentures!" Poole peeks at me and winks. "See, you'll be dead long before that and — "

"I get it. Very funny."

I don't want to turn into a kook. A nut. But Poole whistles happily and I look like a mess. A worm of an idea wriggles into my skull.

"I have a deal for you," I say.

Poole's eyes sparkle.

I pause. "You go to school for me tomorrow, and I'll play your thankful game."

His sparkle vanishes, and for the first time Poole looks sickly.

"Okay, I'll play your thankful game, *and* I'll get you some new boots." I point at his flap-soled pair. "Those look way small."

Poole frowns and bites his lip.

"All right, how 'bout this?" I raise three fingers. "I'll play your thankful game, I'll get you boots *and* a home-cooked meal. Frank probably doesn't cook *that* well, and Mom, well, she's awesome in that category."

"School," Poole repeats.

"There's this girl and I can't seem to talk to her, but I'm running out of time, and I need your help." I exhale hard. "Go to school, get Julia's attention, you know, casually bring me into the conversation. Talk me up, fire some volleys back and forth, and make me sound, well, use some of those smooth words. That's it. The next day I'll swoop in and work my charms."

"You want me to go to school."

"I want you to break the ice with Julia and make me sound unforgettable." I stand up. "Are you scared?"

"I'm not scared, not really, it's more about this uncomfortable rash I get whenever I think about the *s* word." Poole frowns, puffs out air. "One day. I'll go to school one day." He pauses. "Size 10, wide."

"Yeah," I grin. "Wide."

"And lasagna. Does the Owl do lasagna?"

"Extra cheese."

"Yeah," Poole grins. "Extra cheese." He grabs my shirt. "You better keep up your end."

I grimace. "You better take a shower."

He smells a pit and furrows his brow. We walk back to my house in silence. Poole hops into the boxcar, and I head toward my home's back door. I reach it and grab the knob.

"Hey, Martin." Poole swings his feet. "I know things don't look good for you. Eight weeks ain't long. But you are the only Martin right now."

"So?"

"And according to that curse, there always *has* to be a Martin."

"Yeah?"

"Just one Martin?" asks Poole.

"One."

"So unless I'm wrong, since there isn't any other Martin Boyle eating ham sandwiches at your family reunions, at least for these next eight weeks ..."

I freeze, my eyes wide open. "I can't die."

Poole grins and disappears into the boxcar. "Have a fantastic evening!"

Oh, man. If he's right, if I'm right, I could do ... anything.

I feel light, buoyant. I burst in the back door. Mom and Dad stand side-by-side wearing their worried faces. I step up to Mom and kiss her cheek. She reaches for her antibac soap. I move to Dad, raise my hand to high-five him. His stares and slowly presses his paw against mine.

I step back, lift both arms and holler. "I can't die!"

That should count for today's thankfulness.

Mom grabs Dad's arm. "Oh, Gavin, he's delusional. It's far worse than we thought."

"Son," Dad wraps his arm around me. "We need to talk."

"Sure," I say, "but when we do, let's talk fast. I have a lot of living to jam into a little time."

Mom gasps.

"It's fine, Mom. I don't know why it feels fine, but it does. For the first time, I feel great."

"Great?" Mom looks from me to Dad. "Gavin, do something!"

I laugh, clear and free.

The next morning I meet Poole by the boxcar. He sits in the mouth, his left leg bouncing.

"Nervous?" I ask.

"No." He exhales. "Okay, yes."

"Here." I toss him my most oversized clothes. "A couple pairs of jeans to choose from and a T-shirt."

He looks long and hard at the options before snatching ripped denims and disappearing into the blackness.

"How am I supposed to find this girl?" he calls out.

"You won't need to. She'll find you."

"How?"

"You're a new kid." I say, "Everybody gawks at new kids."

"So I'm a zoo animal."

"More or less."

He slowly appears from the dark recesses of the car. He strokes the shirt flat, zips his fly, then fights his hand through his hair. "What do you think?"

I raise my palms and scrunch my face. "Not bad. But that mop on your head. When was the last time you had that cut?"

"Oh no. Hair wasn't in our deal. These are sacred strands, friend, and you ain't puttin' your Germ-Xed hands on 'em."

"Fine." I whip a comb from my back pocket and fling it at him. "Plan B."

Poole pushes the teeth one inch through the brown shag rug. They stick.

"Let me get a scissors." I back toward the house. "Haircuts can't be too hard."

He double fists the plastic handle and yanks some more. It breaks free and Poole screams and stares at the hairball matted in the tines. "I done scalped myself. Forget this, Martin."

"Oh no," I grab his arm and yank him out of the boxcar. "We have a deal."

Minutes later, we walk toward the bus stop. We rehearse for the tenth time. "You'll go to the office and talk to Ms. Corbitt. She's the secretary."

"Office. Corbitt. Secretary."

"Tell her you just moved into the area —"

"Nope. No lyin'. I'm telling her I need to start school."

"Fine. And she'll want to know a ton of information from your parents."

"Covered. Frank, I mean, *Dad*, is meeting me there."

I shoot him a thumbs up. "That's really good. Then you'll get a schedule."

He frowns.

"You know, algebra, phys ed — okay wait, that's trouble. For phys ed you'll need a gym uniform."

"I'm only going one day."

"Halden won't care. I barely escaped The Treatment, and he's in the mood. Okay, listen close. 14 – 2 – 15. That's my locker combo. Locker 121 in the boys' locker room. There's a clean uniform in there."

"14 – 2 – 15."

We reach the bus stop. "Listen. Middle-school survival is tough, but I need you focused on the goal. What's the objective?"

He places his hands on my shoulders. "Find Julia and tell the truth."

I wince. "You might need to be creative with the truth. We're trying to help Julia form a *favorable* impression of me." I jam a folded sheet of paper into his hand. "I've listed all your important duties. Find Julia. Make contact and engage. Look for her table in the lunchroom; it's a good place to get something started. Etcetera."

A distant yellow speck grows. "I'm counting on you, Poole. Find Julia and I'll ... I'll ... be very thankful."

"For what?"

"This favor," I mutter.

"Yell it!"

"I'm thankful that you're doing this for me."

"Scream it, friend!" Poole smacks my arm. "I'm

thankful for Poole the Magnificent and his willingness to do in one day what I've been unable to do in thirteen years! Scream it!"

"I'm thankful that I don't need to endure you today!" I peek at him and grin.

Poole smiles and jumps. "Close enough. I'm gettin' excited, Marty. I'm going to school!" He jukes and spins.

I stare at the bus. "Calm down. I don't need psycho help. I need *cool* help."

I turn and race back toward my house, slip behind a telephone pole and eye the bus stop. Poole still jukes. I slap my face, shake my head.

What have I done?

The bus door opens, and Poole hollers at Father Gooly. "Wow, you're a man of tremendous proportions! How are you today? Do you know a Julia? 'Cause that's my job. See, the name is Poole, and I'm going to school, and there's only one rule, I gotta stay cool, and find the most attractive Julia on behalf of my friend." He spins and does a backflip. "Oh hey, Charley! You ride the same bus? That's helpful because you can help me find — "

The door slams on his voice and the bus pulls away.

I step out from behind the pole, and scuff the sidewalk with my tennis shoe. This seemed like a good idea yesterday, but now my stomach thinks otherwise. *I have unleashed a monster.*

CHAPTER 9

"OPERATION IMPRESS JULIA. PHASE TWO UNDERWAY."
I'm confident — anxious, but confident. If anyone can change Julia's opinion of me, it's Poole.

I shuffle home, my house rising in the distance. My huge, bed-filled, three-shower, toasty-warm house. My empty house. Dad never came home from last night's battle, and Mom was called in to the library.

I glance from my summer home to Poole's. I know Poole said that Frank and the depot guys take care of him, but making a kid sleep on wet wood in a dark box-car is a strange kind of care.

Think, Marty. What would Poole be thankful for?

The thought comes in so quickly, my head aches.

I run to the back door, lift the fieldstone, and grab the baggied house hide-a-key. I slip inside.

"Mom?"

Silence. Good.

I suit up. Elbow-length rubber gloves, protective goggles, and a ski mask. I grab a table knife and walk to the backyard.

Okay, Poole. Let's see what we can do about making life a little more comfortable.

I squeeze behind the evergreen shrub that hides the outside outlet, lower myself into the infested bluegrass, and slice. An hour later, I've dug a two-inch channel from my house to the boxcar. My hands are raw and I'm a mess, but as I search for the fifty foot extension cord, I feel good.

I dash out of the garden shed and press the cord into the channel. I thread one end between a rotted seam in the bottom of the boxcar, plug the other end into our house outlet, and replace the grass on top. Then I tromp it down.

Poole has power. Invisible, beautiful power.

I race inside and check my filthy look in the mirror. I laugh. It doesn't matter —

I'm on a mission. I duck into the main floor storeroom, our personal cemetery for outdated and unwanted appliances.

"Mini fridge ... old microwave ... lamp. And beanbag chair."

I haul out the goods and plug them in, careful to set things far from the visible mouth. A low hum of electricity fills the boxcar.

"Hmm. One more thing."

Back in the house, I grab a laundry basket and head to our fridge. "Apples, oranges, can opener, cans of soup, Spaghettios, ravioli … hot pad."

Soon, Poole's summer cabin is stocked. I smile. It's a start.

I stare at a blank sheet and feel the wind on my face. I'm exhausted from my work. With Mom coming home soon, Poole's outdoor bench will be the perfect place to spend the day and prepare the next installment of *The White Knight*.

I lie on the bench and listen to trains. What would it be like to live here? To wait three years for your mom to come?

Now he's at school helping me out. Definitely worth more than boots and a lasagna.

I spend hours wondering what he'll say when he sees his boxcar thank-you. I think myself to sleep, and I'm still thinking when I wake.

I stretch and sit up and grab my tablet off the ground.

"Poole will break zee ice." I yawn and crack my knuckles. "Martin, zee half-dead love machine, will swoop in with the real continuation of her favorite story." I grab a pencil from behind my ear and blow on the tip.

Oh, Martin, your story and my pictures go so well together! It's like we were made for each other.

"Okay let's see. Where were we ..."

Sadly, the White Knight laid hold of the shaft, raised it to heaven, and ...

Crash!

Shards of clear stone, like daggers of light, exploded into the air. Creatures shrieked and dove for safety, but for many it was too late. Light shattered their armor and they lay in gnarled heaps against dungeon walls.

But not the jackal. Foam dripped from his mouth as he padded among the carnage.

The White Knight backed away, glancing from the wild dog to his stunned adversary.

The Black Knight slowly brought his hand to his chest and touched the gaping wound. Black blood oozed onto his fingers.

He fell to his knees. "Tas," he hissed. "Finish him."

The jackal's eyes gleamed as he limped toward his fallen master. He reached him and licked the blood off his chest. "I hate knights. White or Black."

The Black Knight reached up and grasped Tas by the neck. "I will not be destroyed by a dog!"

Tas crumpled in a furry heap beside his master, and the Black Knight released his grip, collapsing breathless onto his back.

"The prophecy is strong. It has bought you time, young knight." He coughed. "But unless you finish me now, I will be back. And I will claim what is mine." The Black Knight closed his eyes. "Look for me in the heat of summer."

The heat of summer. We're almost there.

The White Knight reached into the rubble and took hold of Alia's hand. He gently lifted her to his side and pulled her close. Her eyes sparkled.

"Behind you!" she screamed.

Tas leaped toward the knight, his jaws clamping around his forearm.

Crack!

"Off, foul beast!" The White Knight pried open its mouth and flung him against the wall. Tas yelped and scampered out of the dungeon.

"Your arm." Alia gently rubbed her fingers over the wound. "It's broken."

"It will heal." The knight smiled. "We are together!"

I set down my pencil. My arm aches from squeezing it so tightly. I rub my forearm and wrist and peek at my watch.

"The time!" I throw down the pencil, slam shut my pad, and bound off the bench. School's out.

I race toward the bus stop, slip behind my pole, and wait. The bus appears and Poole is the first one out. He does another backflip and waves as the bus pulls away. Kids hang halfway out windows and wave back.

"See ya tomorrow, Poole!"

"Do another flip!"

Must've gone well. Wait, where's Charley?

"Well?" I rush up to him. "What did you say about me? What did she say? Did she seem … interested?" I rub my hands together. "You know, did she ask lots of Martiny questions?" I circle him like a yappy terrier. "Say something! You always blab, and now you've gone mute? Speak!"

"Uh, how was your day?" he asks.

"Poole!"

"Oh, right. Our talk. It's a little tough to recall." He turns sober. "I'm thinkin' I should go back tomorrow."

I scratch my head. "So you didn't talk much."

"Not enough. I mean, not enough to do a thorough job."

I grab his arm. "But you did talk?"

He nods.

"A sentence? A minute? What?"

"Pretty much all fourth and fifth hours. She is something. I think another day and we'd know each other pretty well."

"You'd what?" I squint. "Why are my clothes spotted purple?"

He pulls away. "Probably best to leave that detail alone for now."

Minutes of silence drive me crazy. We reach my back-yard and Poole sighs. "Okay, particulars about today," he says. "First off, what's The Treatment?"

My eyes widen. "Why?"

"I went to gym and started to open your locker. Number 120."

"Stop." I exhale hard. "That's Will's locker."

"Found that out. I'm good with names, not great with numbers. So I turn the lock and the door swings open. Must not have been latched. I put on your uniform."

I shake my head. "Will's uniform."

"Right. Will comes in and gets pretty mad, but I tell him the truth. You told me to do it. Seems like first thing tomorrow you need to report to phys ed for your Treatment. Halden said this isn't the first one you've earned."

I tongue the inside of my cheek. "Dead. Officially dead."

"Then there's the matter of a small prune fight at lunch. A rather ... sizable lunch lady escorted me to the office and the principal wanted to see my schedule, but when I dug for it, your note slipped out and —"

"Oh ... What did you tell him?"

"The truth. That I was acting under your orders. That you were sunning, with sunblock, on my bench. He gave us both tickets for some after-school event. Tomorrow, we need to report to reflection, no wait, intention or demention or — "

"Detention." I let my head fall back.

"Yeah! That's it. Go there tomorrow. Here." He digs in his pocket and hands me the slip. "I guess your folks need to sign your ticket. I'll get Frank to sign mine."

My mouth hangs open. I've never had detention.

"Oh, and Charley. There's a small matter with him, but you guys will patch it up. That's most of the big things, I think."

I yank Poole by the shirt and pull him to the boxcar. "In. I want my clothes. You will never go to my school again. Are we clear?"

"But I told Julia — "

"Never!"

He shrugs, and soon purple clothes fly out the boxcar mouth. "This is the way you thank your friend — "

Silence.

Poole appears in the opening, drop-jawed and standing in his boxers.

"Okay, the microwave latch is tricky," I say.

"What did you do?" Poole peeks back into the car.

I frown. "You don't like it?"

"It's just that I haven't uh ... It's been a long time since ..." Poole scratches his head, turns, and leaps. I hear the beanbag chair crunch.

"Love it. Love it." He laughs. "If you ever need another favor, I'm your guy."

I nod and stare at my detention slip. *I don't think so.*

Dad comes home late from the wars. "It was quite a reenactment today." His eyes gleam and he drops his weapon on the floor. "I forgot it wasn't real. I mean, there I was, 1820, arrows flying overhead. Son, there's nothing like it."

I wince and kick at the carpet with my boot.

"Now the tuna is missing. Tuna does not have legs!" Mom's voice carries out from the kitchen. "The macaroni and cheese doesn't either. Gavin, are you feeding the regiment again?"

"Here," I whisper.

I peek at the kitchen and hand Dad my detention slip. He studies it, peeks at the kitchen as well, and whispers back, "You got in a prune fight?"

"A what?" Mom hollers, and slams the fridge. "I assumed that purplage to be the remnants of an art project gone awry. I had already composed a note to Mr. VanSickle. He bears responsibility for the toxic chemicals in those paints. But are you telling me that you ... you were involved in prune hurling?"

"No! Yes. Well, I was really whispering to Dad, not to you."

"Gavin!"

"Your mother deserves to hear the story too." He turns and cocks his head. From behind, I see his body shake. Then Dad breathes deeply, clears his throat, and looks back to me.

"Martin the Prune Hurler."

He can't hold it. He bursts out in a full belly laugh. "Get anybody good?"

Mom slaps him with an oven mitt. "If this isn't proof our son's degenerate behavior ... Oh, Martin. What's happening to you? You will have an appointment with Dr. Stanker this week."

I stare at Dad. He tousles my hair. "Oh, now. Just seems like a kid letting loose a little steam."

He steps back and folds his arms and looks into me. It's a strange look. Not a proud look. A maybe look. A hopeful look. Least that's how it appeared.

"Do we have a purple pen?" He waves the slip in front of my face. "I'll proudly sign this bugger."

Mom storms back into the kitchen. Dad offers a thinking face.

"I didn't hit anybody," I say.

"That's okay. There's always next year."

No, there's not.

CHAPTER
10

I FORGOT TO BE THANKFUL.

I know Poole didn't exactly fulfill his side of the bargain, but I promised. So I stand at my locker and think. Minutes away from The Treatment I think, what in the world do I have to be thankful for?

"I'm thankful that I'm in school and Poole's not."

"Makes two of us, Boyle."

I swing around and stare, nose to hanging whistle, at Mr. Halden.

"Poole's quite a piece of work." He hikes his pants and puffs out his chest. "I just talked with Ms. Jensen. You're spending homeroom with me."

He spins, and I follow. We weave between horrid comments.

"Oooh. Martin's toast."

"Treatment day."

We reach the locker room, go inside, and Halden faces me — his jaw tight and twitchy and terrible.

"Boyle. Since I've known you — I'll be honest — you've been a piece of milk toast. A doormat of a boy."

I bite my lip. "I've been a nice doormat. You know, the kind that reads 'Welcome Home'? Doormats are useful and prevent filth from entering ..." I peek and hope for a smile. Nothing.

"But you defied me with your uniform, you ran out of class, you stole Will's property, and you sent a boy brimming with disrespect to disrupt my well-trained troops. Fact is, you're changing. And I don't like it."

"I've been wanting to change my whole life. You really think I — "

"Your father is a military man." Halden folds his arms. "He understands the importance of a chain of command, and you've reached the end of my chain."

I don't understand what he wants or where he's going. I ease down on a bench.

"Up, soldier!"

I jump to my feet.

"Boyle! On my whistle, march that-a-way."

"Toward the shower room?"

He says nothing. Moments later, Halden's whistle tweets.

I double-time it out of the locker area and approach the showers. Halden strolls through the room, turning each knob until water streams full force from every showerhead. Through the steam, on the far side of the room, he leans against the wall, meaty arms folded.

"Ever played Red Light, Green Light, Boyle?"

"Uh, yeah?"

"Discipline. It's what runs a school. It's what you lack. It's what The Treatment is designed to provide."

He blasts his whistle. It echoes shrilly and painfully off concrete walls. "I call this attitude-corrector Hot Shower, Cold Shower. On my whistle, you jump under the first shower head. It's hot. Then on my next whistle, you jump to the next. It's cold."

"My clothes will get soaked—"

"On my command, you will work your way across the room, and I don't think we'll need to employ The Treatment twice."

"Aren't there maybe some twisted abuse issues involved—"

Tweet.

I leap under the first shower. "Ah!" It's not hot. It's volcano hot. I wriggle and twist and—

"Cold shower!"

I stagger beneath the next showerhead, shirt suctioned to my skin. Ice cold.

"C-cold!"

"Hot shower!"

I stumble through the room of death, my skin alternately burning and freezing. I reach the far end, slump against the cool wall, and stare down at screaming skin — crimsony, raisiny mottled skin.

"Boyle, I don't imagine I'll be dealing with more disrespect."

I shake my head and whisper, "Can I leave?"

He nods. "Hop to. Your dry outfit is on the bench."

I slosh back into the locker room. Halden is nowhere to be seen. But the outfit lights up the room. Bright yellow pants and a neon pink shirt.

Oh no.

The bell rings. Kids will be here soon — I have no choice. I slip gingerly into the shirt and pants and stare at the full-length mirror.

"A dandelion on the bottom and a flamingo on the top." I shake my head. "I'm a Dandingo."

I mope toward the hallway door. The pain. It's worse than Poole's pummeling — every move I make rubs my skin and sets it on fire. Sure, I could tell Creaker, but who would believe it?

I breathe deeply. "All hail the Dandingo!" I push out of the locker room into passing time.

And a circle of kids.

Including Julia.

Will steps up. "Well?" He stares at my clothes. "What happened to you? What's The Treatment?"

The hall hushes and I glance around. Julia's gaze drops mine. "Uh. It's tough."

"But what did he do to ya?" Will presses, and others chorus behind him. Then I see it. They aren't sneering or laughing. They're in awe. I've been through the ultimate torment and lived to tell. For the first time in my life I have something everyone else wants.

Gather round the Dandingo!

"At first when it starts, that's the worst. It builds and builds and inside you want to scream because outside you want to scream, but Halden's a madman, and you know if you show weakness, he'll break you and you'll turn into a puddle, a blob of jello, so you keep going and going and show no emotion, you know, resist giving him any satisfaction. And after you've taken all the pain, all the torment he has to offer, you look your torturer in the eye because you survived The Treatment."

"Whoa!" Will gives me a friendly slap on the back, and nearly knocks my skin off. "Intense." He steps back. "What's with the clothes?"

I freeze. "Oh. That was a calculated move. I woke up thinking, there's no way I'm going to hide today. I need to wear clothes that say, 'Here I am, Halden, come get me, if you dare.'" The lie doesn't sit well, and my stomach turns.

The bell rings, and my circle of admirers scatter like mice. But their words linger.

"Way to go, Martin!"

"Tell me more at lunch. I'll save you a place."

"See ya third hour."

What just happened? Five minutes with a psychotic phys ed teacher and I'm a hero. Julia!

She leans back against a distant wall, hugging her books. In front of her, Charley pleads. From the look on Julia's face, she isn't buying it.

I turn and march to algebra.

"It wasn't me!" Charley's voice screeches, and I glance over my shoulder. Julia shoots the Dandingo a look, and even though she's way down the hall, her eyes warm me more than The Treatment. I smile and pick up my step.

CHAPTER
11

SHE LOVES ME. SHE CAN'T KEEP HER EYES OFF ME. Yeah, yeah!"

The Dandingo spins and poses in the boys' lavatory. Treatment or not, this is officially the best day of my life.

"Martin Boyle, please report to the principal's office. Martin Boyle ..."

I stop spinning, take a deep breath, and trudge toward my doom. Halden's a crackpot, even Mom thinks so. But Principal Creaker? He's different. The old man can make life forever bad.

I open the office door and freeze. Julia sits in the plastic chair.

"Hey, Martin."

The moment has come. Gentlemen, we have contact. It's my turn. It's my moment. Thirteen years of life spent planning the next words that will soar from my mouth.

"Uh-ee." It's a croaky, stuck sound — very donkey-ish. As if the word started out, got jammed in my throat, then blasted out high and girly. It's quite possibly the most ridiculous sound ever made.

Julia laughs. "Do that again."

"Julia? Martin?" Ms. Corbitt clears her throat. "Principal Creaker will see you now."

Julia whispers, "This is where it gets ugly."

I frown and follow her into The Room.

"Close the door, Martin."

I pull it shut. The click is loud and permanent as bone. Suddenly my ears ring, the room tilts, and my vision blurs. I lean into the doorframe, feel its cold against my cheek. It's happening more and more, something scary and sickly.

"No tree hugging, Martin. Sit down, both of you." Principal Creaker removes his spectacles, leans back, and massages his divots. "There can be no confusion as to why you are here."

Julia stares straight ahead. I run my hand through my hair.

"I don't know why I'm here."

"Ah, yes." Creaker leans back. "You weren't here yesterday."

I slump. "Okay. I skipped school. It makes sense that you'd be angry about that, but if you could let *me* break the news to Mom, it would save my life and I promise — "

"If only that were all it was. Martin, do you know how many people went home purple yesterday?"

"Purple?"

"Prune purple."

I glance at Julia. She's trying hard not to grin, but one leaks out. Wow, she's cute.

"I'll tell you. Three hundred fifty-four. Three hundred fifty-four people smacked, walloped, sideswiped, and spattered with prune juice. How does that make you feel?"

"Confused," I say. "I heard something about a food fight but — "

"Let me bring it back for you. 'A gift from Martin Boyle!' Smack. 'A gift from Martin Boyle!' Smack. Yes, your cousin made quite a first-day impression on your behalf."

I push back. "My cousin? Who — Whoa! Poole? Now wait. He does have excellent aim. But I never told him to fire prunes at anyone."

"You didn't send him to school on a mission?"

I grimace. Julia's staring. "Well, I did, but — "

"And did you not tell him to, and I quote, 'fire volleys back and forth with Julia'?"

"I was referring to — "

"Young man, he followed your orders perfectly. Whoever he was. We checked on his address. Number One Boxcar Road does not exist."

Principal Creaker stands. "Do you know what talking to over three hundred angry parents is like?"

I shake my head.

He nods and reaches for his spectacles. "We may never discover where Poole lives, but I welcome you to your new address: the detention room. Your home until I calm down. Slip, please."

I dig the shredded paper from my pocket. "It got wet this morning, but you can kind of see Dad's name there."

Creaker wads the slip into a ball and points to Julia. "And how many times are you going to be in the center of things? Organizing the girls into a prune fighting unit is not the way to end a conflict."

"I was fired upon, sir." She salutes.

Creaker pushes back from his desk, rises, and walks to the window. He stares a good while, before dropping his gaze. "You've already lived through more than a girl should bear, but once again you leave me no choice. You'll be joining Martin after school." Creaker turns. He looks tired. "Am I clear?"

"Yep," she says. "Can we go?"

He shoos us out and we leave the office. Julia turns to me and shrugs. "Looks like I'll be seeing a lot of you."

I nod.

"Who's Poole? He's not your cousin?"

I shake my head.

"You have a hard time talking to me."

I nod again.

"Well, Silent Boy, I'll see you after school." She walks away.

She's getting away.

"Wait!" Finally, a real word! "Here." I dig in my other pocket. "I kept it dry, wrote it for you. I thought you might like to read the next part of the story." I stuff it in her hand and quickstep back to class.

A hero this morning. Julia in the afternoon. Definitely the best day of my life.

I walk into Detention Room 67. It's a room with no windows, not even on the door. Fluorescent lights flicker and buzz like sick flies. Or the sound could be coming from the handful of actual flies bouncing around the ceiling. Either way, this is no place to spend even a fraction of my last couple months.

I walk up to the sour-faced woman behind the desk. I don't know her.

"Hm," she grunts "A newbie. Let's see the pass." She reaches for my wadded admission slip. Her nostrils flare. "You are the prune child. Do you know that your little stunt ruined my daughter's hundred-dollar jeans?"

"No, I uh …"

"Zip it and sit, Prune Boy."

I scan my options and choose a rickety desk toward the back. Words etched on its surface prove this isn't a room for happy, well-adjusted kids. It's a room for the other kind, those who growl through life and don't cover their mouths when they sneeze.

Five minutes later, it's still just Purse-lips and me. I check the clock. Early. I am probably the first kid in history to report early for detention.

May as well work on *The White Knight* while I wait. Let's see ... broken arm. White Knight and Alia finally together.

The White Knight grasped Alia's hand and they fled the enchanted fort.

An hour later, convinced they were out of the Black Knight's grasp, the White Knight ducked into a cave and lit a small fire.

"We could go back to the king, your father. He'll help us."

The knight grimaced. "The citadel is all but empty. He and his army are out fighting in the wars. He won't return for some time."

Alia moved nearer. "Let me look at your arm."

The knight hesitated. "It is not my arm that worries me."

He slowly removed his foot from his boot. Alia gasped.

"What is the meaning of — "

"I do not know." He held his foot nearer the fire's light. "As a baby, it was just a spot, a birthmark on my toe. But the gray rot has spread. The skin is now foul to the thigh, and each day the disease spreads more."

Alia cleared her throat and nodded. "Well then, we will heal what we can. Show me the arm."

Outside the cave mouth, the thunder of hooves.

"Quick, douse the flame. Move deeper in." The White Knight grabbed his sword and rose. "A hoard approaches . . ."

Behind me, the door bursts open and fifteen kids jostle in.

"Assigned seats, everyone!" Purse-lips is hot, but these kids don't seem to care. I look at their faces. These *are* the hard kids. The Tough Kids. The ones who slink around corners of the school where I dare not go. I hear a sneeze and feel droplets of germ-infested spittle coat my neck.

"Hey, Martin!"

Good heavens. A Tough Kid knows my name. He drops down on a knee beside my desk, wipes his drippy nose with his shirt. I'm dead. And that's not supposed to happen yet.

"Way to purple the world, man!" Sniffles flashes the peace sign. "That was art." He grins and stands.

Art? Who are these people?

My bladder throbs. Tough Kid pushes me to an instant bathroom emergency. I stand and walk toward Purse-lips.

"Sit down, Prune Boy."

"But I really need to —"

The door slams behind me. "You made it, Martin. Welcome to my other life."

Julia. I turn toward the door and watch her come nearer.

"Sit over here, Julia."

"Hey, Julia. Saved you a seat."

The Tough Kids know my princess, but she doesn't break stride. She reaches me, grabs my shirt, and stares through me. "We need to talk." She yanks me to an open seat, pushes me into it, digs in her pocket, takes out my story, and slams it down on my desk.

"This story. You wrote it."

I pound my chest and grin.

"So lying to me didn't bother you."

"Uh ..."

"This dumb story has been in my mind for weeks. I have illustrated the entire stupid thing. I have spent hours and hours talking to they-both-said-ouch Charley ... about something he knows nothing about."

"Sit down, Julia." Purse-lips thumps her desk.

Julia drops into her desk. She sits, folds her arms, and seethes.

Think, Dandingo.

The door flies open and the prisoners' heads swivel.

"Where's my Martin?" Mom scans the room, locks

in on me, and scurries to my desk. "Are they treating you well? You look red-faced. Is there fever?"

"Can I help you?" Purse-lips sets down her book and approaches my desk.

"I came to see that my son is treated properly. Can he not be placed in a more healthful setting?"

"No, he can't."

This is an epic clash, two true champions of lip-pursing battling over my desk. Nobody messes with Mom. Nobody can resist that face. I peek up at the detention lady. Her lips quiver. Mom has her on the ropes. One more glare-nostril-flare combination from the Barn Owl and it will be all over.

My defeated captor drops her gaze and slinks back to her desk up front. I try to slump lower but can't. *Show your strength, Dandingo!*

"In that case, I'll be taking him home. He is falsely accused. This whole situation is unfathomable. Come along, Martin."

I close my eyes. I imagine a furious Julia near me, but I don't want to go home. I want to sit right here in solitary confinement because it feels right. I'd rather be close to an angry Julia than coddled by a paranoid mom.

"No, Mom. I want to stay."

Mom leans down. "The air in here is bad. Did you notice there are no vents? I didn't bring the portable air —"

"I want to stay. See you at home." I lay my head on my desk.

She leans over and whispers, "Who has brainwashed you?"

I say nothing. The room is quiet except for that sick-fly buzzing. Finally, my mom's steps shuffle for the door. She gently shuts the latch behind her, and the room comes alive. Laughter. Mocking laughter. I lift my head.

"Knock it off. She's my mom, all right? Just ... knock it off."

I peek at Julia. She shoots me a little smile.

The rest of the hour passes quickly. Purse-lips releases us, and I hurry out the door and down the hall toward the activity buses.

"Martin! Hey." Julia catches up to me, sets down her backpack, and yanks out a portfolio. She pushes it into my chest and hurries away. I don't know what it means and I can't figure her out. But we'll call the exchange progress.

CHAPTER 12

THIS ONE'S A BEAUTY. CHECK IT OUT."

I gently take the sketch from Poole's hands. The explosion of sword on stone and the expression on the Black Knight's face look so real, I blink.

"She's unbelievable," I say.

Poole places the other ten drawings back in the portfolio and leans against the inside of our boxcar. "How you doin'?"

The question feels funny. "With her? I don't know. We're so different. She's always getting in trouble, and I —"

"Go on."

"I never get into trouble, at least I didn't until the cemetery. It's weird now, you know? Days sort of mean more now that I don't have many."

Poole squints and counts the sidewalk-chalk tally on the wall. "You still have plenty, unless the baby comes early, then shoot, you might be living your last."

I feel hot. "Thanks, Poole."

He straightens and brushes off his overalls. "Thing is, this is your chance. What do you want, Marty? More than anything, what do you want?"

"I want Julia to like me."

He points at the pictures. "Done. But what else?"

"I really want to go on a hot air balloon."

"Keep going."

"And I want to join the track team. I always wanted to try that."

"And . . ."

From inside the house, Mom's bell sounds.

"And I'm so tired of being afraid and freaked out every time Mom yells 'germ.' I'm sick of that, you know? It makes me feel so . . . alone."

Poole jumps out and I follow.

"Alone, huh?" asks Poole. "You have me and Julia and shoot, you keep yelling them prayers, I'd say your alone days are over. And you can blow the germ one off too. You won't be alive to get sick." He grins. "Dying does have its silver lining."

"Funny." I march toward the house and for the second time it hits — a lightness because Poole's right. I have two months and my life has changed and nothing I've feared holds me. It's strange to feel good even though I'll kick soon, but at this moment I do. I might be depressed tonight or tomorrow. But I feel free now, and my steps quicken ... and stop.

"Say, Poole. I know you say you're all comfy out here."

"'Specially since I got me a beanbag." He grins.

"Right. But I mean, would you ever want to come over? Like a real kid? Like a normal kid, who sort of comes *from* somewhere and hangs for a while? Or a whole night, if you're sleeping over. Would you ever want to do that?"

Poole stares hard at me. "You're inviting me over."

"I think that's kind of what I did."

He nods. "Your mom—"

"Would see you in the house and die. Yes, she would." I tap my temple. "This is why I'm thinking an overnight. Come really late. Grab a hot shower. Load up on leftovers. Fall asleep on a soft mattress—"

"Sold."

"Then why not tonight?" I ask. "Give me a few hours to work out the details."

Poole tucks in his shirt and flattens the wrinkles. "Better be presentable."

Yes, Mom would die.

I burst in my door.

"Family meeting, son."

I feel good, then bam. Family.

Dad motions me to the couch. Lani and Mom have already assumed their positions in the living room.

Dad cracks his knuckles, sending Mom's eyes a-rollin'.

"I've called this family meeting so we can all voice the concerns —"

"Oh, Gavin, let's get right to the heart of the matter." Mom stands and points at me. "You defied ..."

Dad gently takes hold of her arm and gentles her down into the La-Z-Boy. "Where was I? Concerns. I want us to voice any concerns we may have. And I want to hear from you kids first. Lani?"

My sister glances at me. "I'm good. Martin's a little weird. Everyone at school is talking about him and asking me what it's like to be his sister. But that's okay."

Dad nods. "Martin? Any concerns? Comments? Criticisms? Complaints?"

"I —"

"Go on, son. We're family. You can say anything."

"And you won't get mad?"

He shakes his head.

I look at my seething mom. "I don't want to live like that. All upset and worried. I don't have the time."

Mom licks her lips. "And what is that supposed to mean?"

"I shouldn't have said it. Sorry. I wasn't trying to rip you, I'm just tired of it."

Dad's eyes sparkle. He walks over to me, gently shakes his head, and turns to Mom.

"Honey? Do you have a response?"

Mom leaps to her feet. "I will not sit here while the family rises up in mutiny against my good care." She stares at me. "From your first breath I have watched over you and loved you, and of course, I know those efforts mean nothing to you now that you know it all, now that you no longer need my protective wisdom." She breaks into tears. "But it should. Martin, it should!" Mom scurries toward the stairs.

"Wait!" I dash after her. "I wasn't saying I don't appreciate — "

Her steps quicken and she disappears upstairs.

I descend slowly, look from Dad to my sister.

Lani chews on her lip. "That went well."

"Martin."

Lani's whisper squeezes into my room. I leave my computer and throw open the door to the hallway. "Get up." Sis lifts her head off the floor and crawls inside. I shut the latch behind her.

"Can I come in?" she asks.

I roll my eyes and return to the keyboard. "Let's

see. Midway Regional Bank. Password, password. What would be Dad's password?"

"Prune fights. Detention. Stealing from Dad?" She scoots a chair beside mine. "Mom would say you are moving in a negative direction."

"Mom will not know what I'm doing, will she?" I exhale. "And no, I wouldn't steal from Dad. I'm robbing myself. My college fund." I squint hard. "Any idea about Dad's password?"

"I don't want any part of this."

"Then you should leave."

She folds her hands and her voice drops. "Old soldier."

I glance at her.

"Saw him punch it in one time. It's Old soldier. Capitalize the O."

I enter the account number found in Dad's office and type in the password. Bingo.

"He has six accounts. Oh, here." Martin-Education. I click on the balance tab.

"$22,000 available? I don't need that much. I'll just take two thousand."

"Don't be stupid. Like Dad won't be suspicious if the bank sends him a check for two thousand dollars."

I dig in my pocket and yank out the series of numbers Poole gave me.

"He won't know. I'm transferring to a friend of Poole's who works at the stadium."

"The vagrant? That crazy who came to school? What if his friend keeps it?"

"Wouldn't matter much. What do I need it for anyway?"

Lani leans back. "What's going on?"

I want to tell her about the curse. I want to let her in because she feels more like my sister than she ever has before. She's now my partner in crime and she deserves to know. But I can't. Don't know why, but I can't. If she believed me, she might cry, and I couldn't take that.

"I'm changing life plans, Lani. This may come in handy." I push my hand through my hair and push back from the computer. "College isn't in my future."

"Mom will kill you."

"She can't. It's not possible." I slap my hand over my mouth.

Lani stands and walks toward the door. "You're a different brother. I don't think I know you. I like you, don't get me wrong." She squints. "You're not into D-R-U-G-S?"

I laugh. "No."

She nods, big and slow. "Well, I just wanted to tell you I thought it was great how you answered Mom. Definitely not a loser-answer."

Lani opens the door, peers out, and slips into the

hall. Her head pops back inside. "You didn't hear the P-A-S-S-W-O-R-D from me ... Martin!"

I jump and yank Lani inside, slam the door.

"It's really important that Mom doesn't come in here right now."

She jumps behind me and vice-grips my gut. "The window."

I peer out. A face stares back and I dive to the floor, bringing Lani with me.

Slowly, the window opens and a grimy leg pokes in.

"Hey gang, Marty, Lani. Looks like I got here in time for the fun. What are you playing?"

Lani scrambles to her feet and reaches for the door. I lunge, perform a perfect tackle/hand-slap-over-the-face combination, and again Lani thumps to the ground.

"Don't think I want to tackle Lani all night." Poole tests the firmness of the bed with his hand. "Do you have any other games?"

"Listen," I hiss into Lani's ear. "Poole is over for a sleepover. I'm not sure why he chose ..." — I dagger eye Poole — "the *window* entrance."

Poole jumps on the bed and lands flat on his back. "Thought there'd be less commotion."

I point at Lani. "Yes, this is far less. Thank you."

"No problem."

"So sis, I'm going to let your mouth free and I need it to be quiet. It's a miracle the Owl isn't here already. Can you promise not to make any normal, sisterly, shrieky noises?"

"Mm-hm." She nods, and I slowly remove my palm.

Lani stands and glances from Poole to the open window. "I'm going to my bedroom now. Where doors *and windows* are always locked. I have no valuables except for a clarinet." She peeks at Poole. "You don't play clarinet, do you?"

Poole shakes his head, and Lani tries my doorknob for the third time. "So you'd better stay in *this* room." She slips out the door.

"Well, Poole," I let my arms flop to my sides. "Welcome to my home."

CHAPTER 13

"YOU'VE NEVER HAD A SLEEPOVER?"

I bite my lip and shake my head. I flip through Julia's art. "Nope. Kids less concerned with hygiene ..." I quote Mom and peek at the dusty kid stretched out on my bed. If any kid ever qualified. "... are the carrier pigeons of disease."

"I used to have sleepovers. Eight, nine of us running around my house." Poole grins. "We're probably pushin' the sleepover age limit, but hey, we're making up for lost time. Hand that art over here again."

I hand over a few sheets, stretch out on the floor, and stare at the look on the White Knight's face. He kind of looks like me. "So what now?"

"Typical sleepover? Food. Stupid conversations. Too-loud music. Maybe a movie that scares the wits out of you."

"I haven't done real well here. No cake. Can't play music. No horror flicks." I close my eyes. "Sorry, Poole."

"No friend, you did great. Tackle-the-Lani was fun to watch, and I'm guessing' that there must be something in your fridge." He bounces on the mattress. "And this bed is worth the price of admission."

I sit up. "It's yours for the night. I'll, uh, take the floor." *The germ-infested floor.*

We lie in silence for a minute.

"Say, Marty. We're friends, right?"

"Yeah, absolutely."

"Might be a strange time to mention this, but Julia, she's — "

"Nobody you need to be thinking about." I stand and snatch back her pictures from his hands.

"I'm not. But if ... And don't get this wrong, friend. We'll beat this curse thing." He turns. "But if we don't and you aren't around ... you know what? Forget it."

"No." I say quietly. "You and Julia have that wild side in common. Sounds cool to me. But nothing until I'm — "

"'Course not. Wouldn't think of it."

More silence.

I exhale. "I'll, uh, check the kitchen."

I sneak down the steps and open the fridge. "No lasagna. There. Meatloaf is close."

A quick preheat later, I re-enter my room. "Here, I brought you some ..."

Snore.

"Meatloaf."

Poole sleeps with a smile on his face. No way I'll take that away from him. Probably his first nice bed in years.

I enjoy the late-night snack, shut down the computer, and stretch out on the floor.

Why'd it take a death sentence to get me a sleepover? Why is the only person at my only sleepover a vagrant? Why did said vagrant ask me for his blessing to steal my princess? Nothing in my life makes sense. Not my new-found sister. Not the words I said at the family meeting. Not Poole's disgusting microbials dancing on my sanitized bedsheets.

But I feel good. Having Poole here feels good.

As long as I get him out before 5 a.m.

Sleep doesn't come. Poole, Julia, Death, and barn owls float through my mind's middle world — a land where I'm not quite unconscious, but definitely not awake. It's a place where dreams run free, and at 4:45 I stagger up, exhausted from my adventures.

A shower. Something to wash off the night.

Poole's snore rumbles from beneath the sheets. *Least somebody slept well.*

"Be right back," I whisper, and stumble out toward the bathroom.

Hot water on a cool morning. There's nothing better, and I smile.

Bang. Bang. Distant clangs and a shout.

I shut off the water, poke my head out of the curtain, and reach for the towel.

Poole throws open the door to the hallway, leaps in, and slams it shut behind him.

"We have other bathrooms," I say.

Bang. Bang! The sound nears, and Poole stares at me with wild eyes.

"Barn Owl!" He opens the linen closet, frowns, and throws open the window. "Marty, my friend. Thanks for the sleepover."

"What is going —"

Poole eases himself out, drops silently onto porch shingles. He turns, salutes, and jumps out of sight.

"Can't be good on the ankles," I whisper, and shut the window and wrap with a towel. I open the hallway door.

Smack!

A saucepan smashes my nose, and I crumple to the ground. Mom shrieks. I groan. Lani dashes toward us.

"Oh, Lani. Get me a towel. I mashed Martin!"

A pool of nasal blood forms around my head. I wriggle my nose.

"I'm okay, Mom." I sit and pinch my nostrils together. "If you would've used the Crock-Pot, that'd be different." Mom gapes, and I continue. "If you need the bathroom, next time maybe just knock?"

I smile. Mom purses her lips.

"You have no idea what I saved you from," she hisses. "In your bed, waiting to commit a heinous act, was a ruffian the likes of which you've not encountered."

Lani bursts out laughing. "You were chasing Poo — " She clears her throat. "I mean a ruffian? Catch him?"

"Your levity does not amuse. And yes." Mom glares into the bathroom, lowers her voice to a whisper. "He's hiding in that bathroom. Do not worry children ..." Mom rises, steps quietly — cat-like — then screams toward the linen closet.

I stand and walk back down the hall with Lani. We turn to see Mom slump to the floor, all a mutter. "In the bed. He was in Martin's bed. Then down the stairs, into the study. He hopped Gavin's desk. Into the kitchen. Back upstairs. Into this bathroom. I saw it ..."

My face throbs, and I draw my towel tighter around myself.

Lani bumps my shoulder. "One sleepover is probably all you need."

CHAPTER
14

H ALLELUJAH! THANK YOU FOR THIS MELTY BUTTER
dripping down my pancakes!"

Lani jumps and drops the Aunt Jemima onto the
floor. I should have warned her, but I wanted to get my
primal thankfulness yell out of the way early.

"What was that for?" She swallows hard.

I shrug and stuff a bite in my mouth. "I was just — I
mean, pancakes without melty butter?" I lift the butter
dish and inspect it closely. "What good are they, right?"

"Right," she says slowly.

I finish and carry my dish to the sink. "Where's
Mom?"

"Back in bed." Lani yawns. "She called in sick to the
library. The locksmith is on his way to change all the
locks."

I chuckle, drop my dish with a clank, grab Julia's
pictures, and race out toward the bus stop.

"Top of the mornin', Martin." Father Gooly squints. "Appears you took a blow to the face, lad."

I shrug at Father Gooly and hop up the steps. He grabs my arm and I lean in.

"What might be going on with Charley? He bears the look of dead veal, don't cha know. Won't say a word to me."

I pull free and hobble down the aisle. Sure enough, there's a sickly looking veal slumped in the backseat. I ease down beside him.

"Don't!" Veal springs to life and shoves me back into the aisle. "Don't even think about planting that ugly face there. Take the seat behind me."

"But there isn't a seat — " I plop down again, and the bus clunks forward. "What's up?"

"It would be nice if we could just pretend that everything was an accident. But it's no good, Marty. My old best friend Marty. Snake-in-the-grass Marty. Weasel Marty."

I sigh and let my head fall back against the seat. "For my sake, humor me. Make believe I know nothing, okay?"

"'I wrote a song so the world will know, how Martin's friend feels about Julia Snow.' Do I need to go on?"

"You wrote her a song?" My face scrunches. "You can't sing."

"No kidding. That was a nice touch. You outdid

yourself. But did you have to play it in the girls' locker room? Why, Martin?"

My jaw drops. "I didn't write a song. I didn't sing a song. I don't know who wrote ... I do know who wrote it. Poole."

"Boxcar boy?"

Charley puts on his thinking face. That's tough for Charley so it takes a while, but two minutes later his eyes light up. "He's the friend. Poole was talking about himself."

"He's the friend."

"But I'll never be able to speak to Julia again. I knew that kid was trouble the first time I saw him."

I look away from Charley and grin. Poole messed up my life, but the more I think about it, his visit was pretty effective.

I get to school and weave toward the health department. Same kids. Same halls. But today I'm the zoo animal. Martin, Treatment, Psycho Mom, Julia — the words are everywhere. But I can't slow down. I'm on a mission to find the health teacher, Coach Murphey. I gently open his classroom door and peek inside.

"Coach?"

The big man jumps, and his life-sized skeleton rattles

and clanks to the floor, its bones piling in a plaster heap. Coach turns, a skull left in his hands.

"You don't want to know how long it took to piece Old Ruthie together."

"No, I don't." I slip in and the door slams behind me. The pelvis jiggles off its pole and clatters to the floor with the rest of the bones.

Coach tongues the inside of his cheek. "Now that you have my undivided attention, what can I do for you?"

I breathe deeply. "I want to join the track team."

"The track team." He rubs his face, looks at the skull. "The boy wants to join the track team. What do you think?" He holds Ruthie's jaw up to his ear. "Uh huh. I'll ask." He glances at me. "What event are you interested in?"

"What events are there?"

Coach rolls his eyes. "Sprints. 100 meters. 200 meters. 400 meters. Distance events and hurdles." He bends over and picks up the pelvic bone.

"I don't run fast. Do you have anything else?"

Coach waves me over. "Help me find the vertebrae."

It's worse than touching a bat — Ruthie and I have too much in common.

Wonder if I'll hang in a classroom someday.

"Let's see, we only hold a few field events in middle school. You'll have to wait until high school for all the choices."

No, I won't.

"There's the long jump and the high jump."

"All jumping, huh?"

Coach points at me with a rib. "Are you sure you want to go out for track?"

"Okay, which event has the fewest athletes?"

"Easy. Hurdles. Hand me that femur, would you?" He snaps it into place. "I don't have a single hurdler at 300 meters. We take an automatic disqualification in that event in every meet. What would you say to that?"

"That's more jumping."

"And running. Double whammy for you." Behind us, Coach's homeroom begins to fill. "What do you think?"

I look at the skeleton, my destiny. "I'll take it."

Coach smiles, walks me to his desk, and hands me a waiver. "Get this signed by a parent or guardian and show up Monday right after school."

"I'm experiencing a little detention issue — "

He looks at me hard and then pats my back. "Come to the track. I'll see if I can't get you out on parole."

I don't see Julia until detention. She comes in quietly; sits beside me quietly; twiddles her fingers quietly. I twiddle mine too.

After a minute of finger exercises, she pounds the desk, turns, and glares. "Well? What did you think of them?"

I bend and gently extract her portfolio from my backpack. I lay it on her desk. "Never seen drawings so good." I point at my nose, Mom's facial artwork. "I was staring at them so hard I tripped and smashed my face. They're awesome."

"You're right, they are." Her glare turns into a grin. "That story is pretty good too."

"Pretty good? It's better than that. It's awesome!"

"You're right. It is."

Purse-lips shushes us, and I watch another hour of my life vanish. But Julia is here so I won't complain.

I'm thankful I'm in detention.

The voice is my own. I hear it in my head, which makes no sense. I already kept my bargain today with the syrup scream. But looking at Julia's smile, I can't deny it — I am thankful. Really.

We walk together to the activity bus. "What are you doing after school?" she asks.

"I have an errand to run at Midway Stadium."

"A family errand or an alone errand?"

"Alone, I guess."

"Want some company? I told Lucy I'd be home late."

I frown. "Lucy's your mom?"

"I wish." She kicks at the ground.

I shrug and feel butterflies flutter in my gut. They're wrestling or dancing or doing whatever butterflies do when they have a party. "Yeah, I'd like company."

Ten minutes later, we hop off near my house. We walk the tracks, our arms outstretched. She's a good balancer. I'm not. Every three steps I fall off my rail and our hands bump. I don't mind falling off my rail.

"Who's Lucy?"

"Foster mom number two." She falls off and stops. "Way better than foster mom number one."

I say nothing.

"I was in third grade. The principal called me to his office. There were three adults waiting there and they all wore you-poor-thing faces." She shakes her head and breathes deeply. "I ran out before they could tell me what I already knew. Motorcycle accident." She forces a smile. "Whenever I'm back in Creaker's office I sort of feel close to both of them. Like they're still here, laughing and smiling. Is that weird?"

"No," I whisper.

She tosses back her hair. "But who cares, right? It's history. Where are we going?"

"I don't think you'll understand."

"Try me."

We squeeze between the outfield fencing and walk the warning track.

"It starts with my name. It's cursed." I peek at her.

"Which one?"

"Which what?"

"Which name?"

"Oh, my first. But kind of my second too. I'm coming to that part."

I tell her about the cemetery, the ceremony, the pattern. I tell her all about Poole. I remind her that words have power. Then, I wait — for minutes.

"Aren't you going to say anything?" I ask.

"Nope."

"You don't believe any of it."

"Nope."

We walk into the home field dugout and sit.

"But you have a wild imagination. No wonder you write so well. That'd make a good movie — "

"Yeah, it would. I could star as Poole." A head pops down from the top of the dugout. "Hey, you two." The leprechaun flips down onto the field. "Nice to meet you again, Julia."

She nods slowly. "You don't really live in a boxcar behind Martin's house?"

Poole bites his lip. "Is that what Marty told you?"

I flash him my squintiest look, and he raises both hands in surrender. "Okay, yeah, but only during the summer months. I've had my eye on some used furniture. The place needs a girl's touch, someone with an eye for artistic design. You should come by to see — "

I kick him in the shins. "… Martin. To see Martin. That's right, just toss Poole the leftovers." He rubs his leg, scowls, and points. "Here comes your bank."

Poole hobbles toward the equipment door. An old guy limps out. He looks friendly enough — dirty clothes, work boots, no front teeth.

You know, periodic dental visits could have prevented gingivitis and you might still have those — be quiet, Mom!

"So this is Martin. Name's Frank." It's a gravelly introduction, as if he just swallowed a mouthful of infield. "Transferring all that cash? You're a very trusting kid."

"There aren't many options," I say.

Frank digs in his pocket, retrieves a bank envelope, and slaps it in my palm. "Better count 'em."

I set the hundreds on the bench and Julia's eyes grow big.

"$1,800. $1,900 … Hey, I'm short!"

Frank laughs and reaches into his shirt pocket, extracts one last bill. "Just toying with you, kid." He glances around the ballpark all nervous-like. "I'm leaving before someone sees this little transaction. Looks mighty illegal."

Frank totters away; Poole winks at Julia and follows. Finally we're alone, and silence lands heavy. I don't want to move. I want to sit right here with Julia and my two thousand dollars. But the quiet gets all weird, so I stuff the money in the envelope and into my pocket.

"What are you into?" Julia asks.

"I told you. I'm cursed and — " I face her square. "Let me prove it."

I lie in bed awake. *How do you convince someone you're dying?*

I throw off the covers. She needs proof. Evidence.

The White Knight rests on my bedstand. I reach over, flick on the lamp, and grab the notebook.

Beneath me, I hear pounding in the kitchen. Mom and Dad must be having a Discussion. Strange, their talks used to make me wince. But Poole's parents are gone. Julia's parents are gone. I guess just hearing your parent's voices is a reason to be thankful.

"Back to the cave. Okay, a hoard approaches."

The White Knight crept to the cave mouth, his sword at the ready.

Outside, the sound of dismounting and the clink of approaching armor.

The knight stepped out of the shadows. Twenty knights bearing the Aurel crest, the crest of Alia's family, bowed low to the ground.

"Rise, friends." The White Knight exhaled. "How did you find us? Do you have news?"

Lonelyn, the Aurelian commander, slowly rose. "Dire, sir. May I speak to the princess?"

The White Knight stared into the commander's unblinking eyes. "Alia? Come out."

Alia came forward, her jaw fixed. "Speak, man."

Lonelyn bowed low to the ground. "Your parents, the Aurelian king and queen, have been murdered."

Alia grabbed the White Knight's hand. Her voice quavered. "By whose hand?"

"It is not known. But we have been sent to find you. The king and queen will be laid to rest tomorrow." Lonelyn rose and grabbed the reins of two horses. "You must come. Aurel needs a leader, princess. That position now falls to you."

Alia looked to the White Knight.

"The decision is yours, my lady."

Tears streamed down her face. "I will come to the cemetery, but only if the White Knight accompanies me."

"Of course, princess, thus the two horses ..."

I set down the pad. Of course. The proof Julia needs. It's in the cemetery. But the getting there.

I look around my room.

Two horses short.

CHAPTER
15

"DAD, THIS IS JULIA."

Dad peers over the newspaper, raises his eyebrows at me, and extends a hand to my guest. "Hello, young lady. I take it you're a student at Midway."

She nods and looks around our living room. I make a frantic search for photos of bruised body parts. Looks clear.

"Whose voice is that? Have they been offered antibacterial handsoap?" Mom comes out from the kitchen and pauses. "I've seen you somewhere. I never forget a face."

"She's right," I whisper. "Like a barn — "

"If you've something to say, speak up. Whispering in front of others is the first step toward delinquen — That's it!" She walks to Dad's side and hisses, "This girl is a delinquent. She was in detention."

"So was your son," says Dad.

"That was *your* son. My son is careful and considerate and has, apparently, vacated the premises. I thought, perhaps, our family meeting was an aberration. But I've not received a single thank-you for saving his life from the I-N-T-R-U-D-E-R. See ..." She points at my nose. "Proof of my love."

"Like I was saying, this is Julia, and I need a favor. Now that I think of it, two favors." I glance from Mom to Dad. "Probably from Dad."

Mom stomps back to the kitchen. Julia leans over. "If this is trouble for you, I don't need to go. It's no big deal."

"It is a big deal. You believing me *is* a big deal." I face Dad and take a deep breath. "Tomorrow is Saturday and you don't work and I don't work so we're both free. And Julia doesn't live with her parents but she does live with a foster parent who is trying to get her to meet nice kids at school. And I'm a nice kid and you're a nice dad so we qualify. And Julia loves to four-wheel, and we don't have a four-wheeler, but Uncle Landis does. And I kind of got the bug for them last time I was there, and so I was wondering if tomorrow you would drive Julia and me to Uncle Landis's place and we could ride and you two could talk or kill stuff."

I gasp for air and peek at Dad. He's staring hard at me, a trying-to-figure-me-out stare.

"Oh, and this." I dig in my pocket and pull out the

crumpled waiver from my track coach. "If you could sign, that would be great."

"More detention, eh?" Dad grabs the sheet and a pen from his shirt pocket and scribbles without reading. "You *want* to go to Landis's?"

I snatch back my waiver and wait. He rubs his face. "Absolutely. If you want to go, and it's fine with Julia's foster parent, then absolutely."

Crash.

Crash.

Pots hit the floor in the kitchen.

Dad smiles at Julia. "Don't worry about Martin's mom. She's getting used to having a teenage boy."

Saturday wakes up misty, with air thick like pea soup. Dad and I hop into the Suburban, plug Julia's address into the GPS, and pull out onto Industrial Boulevard.

"She's seems like a right nice young girl, son."

"She is a right nice young girl."

Dad pauses. "You know, we've never really had the chance to, well — we've never directly spoken about nice young girls. I mean, I saw how you *were* and always reckoned I'd have a bit more time, but seeing how you *are*, I'm thinking this may be as good a time as any."

Not the Talk.

"Could we not talk about this right now?"

"You need to know about the changes that come over a boy about your age. It's my job to — "

"You know, you're right. We should have that talk."

"Yeah?"

"Because I have lots of questions," I say.

"You do?"

I nod. "But it will take a while to gather my thoughts. Can you give me a couple months?"

"A lot of mischief can happen in a couple months. Why, your mother — "

"Stop! That's just disgusting." I shake thoughts of Mom and Dad from my head. "I just need gathering time."

Dad quiets, turns toward me, and lays his heavy hand on my shoulder. "If you say so. A few months it is."

I'm thankful I'll never have to endure the Talk.

We reach Julia's place. Lucy comes out and meets Dad. At first, they're distant, like two circling dogs who don't trust each other. But soon, suspicious sniffing turns to laughing and Lucy lets Julia hop in back.

Dad writes down his cell number and hands it to Lucy. "I'll have her home by supper."

"Julia, take my cell. And Mr. Boyle, you'll be with the children?"

"I'll be on the farm the entire time." Dad closes Julia's door.

"Wait!" Julia pushes back out and disappears inside the house. She reappears holding a sketchpad, races toward us, and hops back inside.

"It's my latest *White Knight* drawing. I drew it last night. You can't look at it now, with me here." She sets it on the seat. "Tonight when you get home, okay?"

I nod, Lucy waves, and we back down the driveway. Wilderness, here we come.

The trip goes quickly. Dad entertains us with stories of blowing people up at Fort Snelling. Julia laughs and giggles like I've never seen her laugh and giggle.

"So, Dad." I lean into his shoulder. "How long until we get—"

"There's nothing like the scent of gunpowder after a man repels a ferocious attack." He peeks at his audience in the rearview.

I interrupt. "Do you think Landis will be ho—"

"Last year, we were surrounded on all sides. British. Indian tribes. We brought out the big guns," says Dad.

Giggle-giggle-gasp from the backseat.

"You know, a few years back I watched Charley blow up firecrackers," I offer.

Dad continues, "Body parts flying, guts oozing."

"Technically," I say, "those firecrackers are illegal in Minnesota. Pretty intense!"

Dad puffs up. "I let loose from the battery, and their lead man's head flew right off!"

Laugh, laugh, laugh. Julia's doubled over.

I lose.

We jerk right and slosh through Landis's mud driveway. Dad fishtails to a stop in front of the farmhouse.

Landis smashes out the front door, rifle in hand.

"Who done come onto my — Brother! Here's a surprise. Shoot. You bring the rest of the brood?"

"Half a brood," he calls. "I have Martin, and Martin has a friend. This is Julia."

"I'll be. Marty has a friend indeed. You know Marty, I remember when you was ..." He lifts his hand to his waist. "... yea high. Now you done found yourself a lady friend." He looks at Dad. "Time flies, does it not?"

"It does indeed."

"Where's my manners? Step inside." He waves toward the door. "Jenny's 'bout to skin a rabbit for some stew. Bugger's still kickin'. If you like, I'll hack off the foot. It'd make a lucky gift for your somebody, Martin."

"Uncle Landis, if it's okay with you, we'd like to go four-wheeling."

He points his rifle toward the shed. "You know where I keep the equipment. Keys're inside. Have at it."

I flash Julia a weak smile. If I don't scare her away, somebody in this family sure will.

She runs toward the shed and shoves open the door. "Polaris! Awesome." Julia hops on the red one. The engine snarls and roars. "Race you, Marty!" She cranks it in reverse, spins a neat backward circle, and explodes out into the mud.

I cough and chew my nails and stare at the three green ATVs. "Race you, huh? Okay." I approach the nearest one. "Hello, loud, fast machine. I'm Martin." I gently lift my leg over. "Remember, right now I can't die. So go easy."

I turn the key and my engine fires. I double-fist the stick. "P for Park. R for Reverse." I yank the stick and flutter the gas. The ATV jerks backward. "Whoa. Easy boy." I slowly back out of the shed. "D-Drive."

"Can't die. Can't die." Gas! I fly forward. My feet fly up and catch beneath the handlebars. The machine slows, and I stare at the little thumb switch thing.

Slap!

"Ow!" I grab at the back of my head as Julia flies by me. She's lapped me and slapped me. Not acceptable.

I have a thumb war with the handle grip, take a deep breath, and squeeze.

"Cripes!" Twenty, then thirty miles per hour. I bounce and slosh and mud splats on my glasses.

"Yee-haw!"

My holler and my smile come from nowhere, and I can't stop either one. I wait for the wave of guilt that always comes after really big smiles, but there's nothing — nothing but thick, wet, soupy, muddy screams I didn't know my throat could make.

I listen for Julia's four-wheeler. Martin Boyle is ready to ride. Martin Boyle is ready to rumble. I zip up the hill and jerk to a stop.

Julia's machine rests alone. She stands frozen in the cemetery, her eyes on the tombstones. I walk up beside her and together we stand in silence.

"I wouldn't have lied to you. Do you see — "

"Shut up. Just shut up!" She runs out of the graveyard, runs down the hill, and out of sight.

I walk to my spot, the patch of earth next to my uncle. I lie down, my face in the dirt, and cry.

CHAPTER

16

"Have you seen Julia?" My eyes still sting.

Jenny rocks in her chair and smiles. "She ran in, then ran out. She seemed quite upset both ways. Your dad and Landis are out looking for her. Oh!" Jenny stretches out her hand. "Come over here. Quick."

I shuffle toward her and bend down. "You okay?"

She beams. "He's kicking again. Here." She grabs my wrist and presses my hand against her belly. "Feel that?"

Inside of my aunt, a boy kicks hard, and my hand jerks away. "It's okay." Jenny gentles it back. "In a few weeks, you'll be spending a lot of time with this tyke. Oh! Did you feel that? Your cousin wants to play with you."

He wants to kill me.

I gulp. My cousin. He pushes and kicks and jumps inside my aunt. He's getting ready for life, growing stronger by the day. My knees weaken.

I pull my hand away and offer a weak smile. "That's uh ... that's something."

Aunt Jenny rubs her stomach and starts to hum. I need to get out of here.

The screen door bangs open.

"We bagged the girl." Landis strides in and places his gun on the rack.

"You were hunting her?" Thoughts of Martin the deer fill my head.

He laughs. "No. Just habit. Never know when I might come across dinner for my Jenny and my great big beautiful boy!"

I back out the door. Dad stands by our Suburban, his forehead furled. Julia sits in the backseat, her head in her hands.

"Do you have any idea what happened, Martin?"

I don't answer.

Dad exhales and reaches his arm around me. His voice softens. "Okay."

I slip in the front seat.

Julia sniffs and rocks, and I don't know what to say.

"It's not fair," she whispers. "It's not fair. Why did you write me that stupid story? Why did you ever start talking to me? I never asked to know you."

"Sorry," I say.

Dad hops in and we drive home in silence. We drop

her off and she exits without a word. Dad glances over at me. "You didn't do anything to her, did you?"

My head thuds against the window. "More than you know."

"Psst. Martin."

Lani steps into Dad's office. It's midnight on Sunday, a school night, which means the Barn Owl wants us both in bed.

"Stealing more passwords?"

I grin and set down my pencil.

"I heard Dad talking to Mom." She quietly closes the French doors and sits down. "What happened with Julia?"

I look at her and sigh. I've never liked Lani. She's been a little sister, which by definition means she's an irritant. Something between a gnat and a mosquito. But for the second time in a few days, I wish I'd spent more time with her. She doesn't steal my stuff or sneak into my room. Lani wouldn't make the sister hall of fame, but she's pretty okay.

"Nothing happened." I drop my gaze. "Except it sounds like I got Mom and Dad talking. You know, whatever happens, I think you've been an adequate sister."

"Now you're scaring me." She stands up to leave and pauses at the door. "I guess you're adequate too. But don't think I'm going to get all blubbery or make you cookies or do your chores just because you called me adequate." Lani scurries out of the room and up the stairs. "It's not even much of a compliment," she yells down. "Sort of between okay and acceptable, and neither of those is magnificent. Now that would have been a compliment — magnificent. Lani the Magnifi ..."

I sigh again and nestle into Dad's big chair. "Okay, where was I ... *A murder in Aurel. The knight and Alia on the way to the funeral.*

It was a silent procession toward the kingdom of Aurel. Alia grew increasingly nervous as the royal cemetery came into view.

"Lonelyn. Where are the mourners? Is there nobody to weep?"

"Nobody, save this detachment, knows of the murders. The news would lead to chaos. Had we not found you, our enemies would certainly have attacked our leaderless kingdom."

Alia nodded and rode beneath the iron arch. The White Knight galloped to her side.

"Do not dismount," he whispered.

She frowned. "Why not?"

"Can you not feel it? The darkness of this place?"

"Of course. A great evil has been done."

The knight's horse reared and calmed. "Yes, but this evil feels familiar."

"We are here to mourn the passing of the king and queen," a cloaked man called from the opposite end of the cemetery. "And to witness the passing of the White Knight!"

The cloak fluttered to the ground and the Black Knight laughed. "Seize them."

"A trap." The White Knight slapped the rear of Alia's horse. "Ride! I will follow!"

The two thundered between the tombstones, twenty riders close behind.

"When we reach the river, veer south, I shall head north. Farewell, Alia."

"No, you are beyond cruel! It would be better for me had you left me safe in the stone. How can you free me only to abandon me?"

"I don't want this. But it will be better for you. The Black Knight will not stop searching for me. You must believe— "

The White Knight gave Alia's horse a kick, and it galloped into the southern woods. The knight splashed into the shallows, faced downstream, and rode until his horse could push no more. He dismounted and walked until he reached a hut of straw and mud.

"Hello?"

Nothing.

The knight entered and collapsed. The pain in his thigh had worked its way to the hip.

"I don't want this. I don't want to live alone." He rubbed his side. "Why is this happening to me?"

"Then fight your enemy, you fool!"

From the corner, a small voice, old and brittle.

"Who goes there?" The knight drew his sword.

"Oh, just put that down." An old man with tattered clothes struggled to stand. "You want to live. Then do it, man. Fight."

The knight stepped toward him. "I can't beat this enemy."

"You are afraid to try."

The words pierced his armor; he knew them to be true. "I am afraid to fail." His hip throbbed. "If you knew what ailed me—"

"What about the woman?"

The White Knight straightened. "How do you know of her?"

"It's always a woman. Doesn't she deserve more from her knight?"

Alia deserves it. I deserve it.

The knight struggled to stand. "She does, indeed."

"Remember young man, words have power."

I throw down my pencil. "Poole, get out of my story." I reread the page. I remember Julia. For her, for me, I want to fight. I want to live.

I'm up all night, trying to Google my way out of this curse. I'm stuck. I'll need help. Poole's help. Julia's help. Anybody's help.

Morning finds me flat on my back — a Martin-shaped floorboard. I toss a baseball up, palm it when it drops.

Up and down.

Up and down.

"Come out of your room, Martin. It's time to get you some help."

"Sorry, Mom. I'm kind of busy."

Up and down.

Mom bursts in. She sees me and gasps. "Parasites. If you could see the millions of parasites that cover the floor — "

"Can you see them?" I ask.

Up and down.

She taps her toe and checks her watch. "I made you an early appointment with Dr. Stanker. You may continue your unsanitary activities after we return."

"I don't want to see him. I don't need rest." Up and down. "I want to go to school."

"Not in your condition. Come." She takes three steps down the stairs, turns and motions to me. "Come!"

I exhale long and slow. Up and dow — "Ouch!"

Maybe we can talk about the divot in my head.

I trudge to the car and throw my pack into the backseat.

Julia's drawing. Forgot all about it!

I grab the sketchbook and set it on my lap. Better to examine it at the doctor's office. If I ooh and aah now, it'll just be more questions from Mom.

We arrive at Dr. Stanker's office building. It's bleak and drab. A lot like detention, without Julia.

"Now Martin, I know that you haven't always felt … comfortable with me." Mom pauses at the elevator and her gaze drops to the ground. "I suppose I can understand some of that."

I blink. It's the most human I've ever seen Mom. No Barn Owl in her. It's almost a normal, nice thing she just said and I don't know what to do with it, so I turn and stare at the up button.

"But I want you to feel free to open up during your session. Tell him anything." She grabs my arm and I peek at her. "It's just not normal for you to smile so much. We need to get that insidious urge under control."

Mom's back.

"Right," I say. "I'll open up for one hour."

We hop on the elevator.

"Dr. Stanker is an old friend of your father's. He specializes in death, death obsessions, death fixations, death fetishes …"

The door opens and I jump out, Mom spewing Death behind me.

"… death manifestations, death—"

I knock on the door to Stanker's suite; Mom fires her hand into her pocket and squirts my knuckles with hand sanitizer. She's like Jesse James.

I wipe gel off my fingers and the sketchbook. "I'm going to buy you a holster for Christmas. At least I would if I was around — "

"What's that? What were you just going to say?"

The door swings open. "Welcome, Martin, no need to knock. There's a waiting room inside." The exceptionally cheery receptionist smiles at me. I smile back, turn, and smile at Mom.

She scowls and shakes her head. "This will take deep therapy. Mark my words."

"Mahtin, Mahtin Boyle?"

"It's Martin."

"Yeah, yeah, Gavin's boy. Come in."

Dr. Stanker must be from New Yoke or New Joisey, and I can hardly understand him.

"Sit. Sit." He points at a couch. It looks comfy, but it's cold to my hands.

He takes a seat on another couch, grabs a manila folder, and squints.

"It says here, you plan on dyink soon." He peeks at me. "Speak to me."

I peek at the end table, reach for the thick book that rests there.

Death and You.

"Yep, I do. We're down to under two months, and I, Martin Boyle, will be in the obituary page. Knowing Mom, I'll be in color; you might want to keep an eye out."

"Wonderful, wonderful." He wrings his hands in delight. "And how do you plan on dyink?"

"You have some trouble with your g sounds."

"Just answer the question."

"I can't." I rub my head. "I don't know how that part works. And I've been spending a lot of time thinking about that. I mean, will I just fall asleep? Will my heart just run out of beats? Will I *mysteriously* fall down a hole or *happen* to get run over by a truck? Or let's say I never leave my house. What if I sit in the hospital lobby holding Mom's danger bell? What would happen then?" I lean forward. "Have you ever died before?"

"No, I don't imagine I have."

"See that's just it. You're clueless too, no offense." I lie down. "If you knew anything about curses, now *that* would be helpful."

"Coises? I'm from Boston, home of the Red Sox. And the boy asks if I know about coises."

I leap to my feet and raise my hands to heaven. "I'm now thankful for this curse expert!"

I smile sheepishly and ease back down. My shrink sets down his pad and stares.

"Sorry," I shrug. "I forgot to scream today. It's a prayer."

"This is a prayer? Do you think God is deaf?" He rubs his right ear and winces. "That was a thankfulness scream. Why are you thankful? You'll be dead in eight weeks."

Again, I rise and walk slowly around his office. "I don't know. But seems like I really am, like it's more than a bargain I made with Poole. I can't stop thanking. For Poole and Julia and Dad and Lani and sometimes Mom and now for you, my curse guru."

He frowns. "A boy who yells his prayers."

"What I told you." I catch his gaze. "I'm making up for lost time. I didn't pray before. Now that's interesting." I scratch my head and restart my walk. "Why thank God now? I mean, I'm mad at him too. Can you be mad and thankful at the same time?"

He straightens his glasses. "Let's get back to the death fetish — "

I pause. "No way. I'm doing deep therapy here. Can you be mad and thankful at the same time?"

"Yes. Now regarding death — "

"That settles it. I'm thankful and mad. It's possible. There's a nugget you can share with your other shrin-kees. Now, about the curse — "

I spend the rest of my time explaining my wretched condition. He doesn't say or write a word. He sits and eats mints, little pastel pillow-shaped mints that grandmas have on coffee tables.

"If she delivers on time, I figure I have about two months."

He taps his temple. "You don't want to die, do you?"

"Of course not," I say.

He rolls his eyes, stands, and throws my file in the garbage. "Why did your parents bring you here? You don't need help with dyink, you need help with livink."

I bite my lip. "Yeah, you're right."

"Here's what you do, kid." Dr. Death thrusts his raised pointer in front of my nose. "First, accept it. So you're coised. We all are; you should meet my in-laws. But with coises, you got to find out where they started."

"Where they started."

"Yeah, where they started. For me, I should have known when Irene's mother first looked — find where this coise started and then undo it."

"Undo it."

"Sure, undo it. Unless it's an in-law, then you just keep — yeah, undo it."

I stroke my chin. "You can do that?"

"Sure, kid. Whatever. If I can live through Irene's mother, you can live through anything."

"I think this is a little more complicated than your mother-in-law."

"You listen." Dr. Stanker leans forward, toting some serious anger-management issues. "We'd been married one day, one day! We were on our honeymoon. Irene looked beautiful. And her mother ..."

I glance down at the sketchbook. I flip to the seventh page and stare.

In the center of the new drawing, a baby, held by his father. Proud men in robes and men in armor encircle the pair, each one laying a hand on the tiny child. And in the back, drawn so gray and black he almost fades into the castle wall background, is a sinister face I know well from the other sketches. His hand grasps the baby's toe.

"The Black Knight," I whisper.

"... you can be certain," Stanker continues. "It was a very black night ..."

I squint hard. Beneath Julia's scene, she had penciled a small caption.

The "Blessing" of the White Knight.

"... so I tell Irene, our marriage is one day old and your mother has already cursed it ..."

I rub my fingers over the child. *That's me. I'm the White Knight. A hero cursed from birth.*

I jump up.

"But you said I can undo it!"

Dr. Death scratches his head. "Oh, your little coise situation. Yes. Find the start and undo it."

Find the beginning. Find the Black Knight.

I grab the sketchbook and squeeze it to my chest. "Julia, you're a genius."

I shake the doctor's hand, hard. "You don't know how much you helped me."

"Glad to be of assistance. When you feel like dyink, then you come back and we'll talk."

I throw open the door into the waiting room, a smile so wide I feel it on my face.

"Oh, doctor!" Mom stands up. "What have you done?"

"Hi, Mom! Get me to school! I have a lot of work to do. It's time to start Operation Save Martin."

"Martin." Mom's fingers whiten on the steering wheel. "Are you listening to me? What did the doctor say to you?"

"Hang on."

He's talking to the old guy, blah, blah, okay.

"But how can I defeat an unknown enemy? This knight in black? Where does he come from? How does he draw his strength?"

The old man gestured to the single chair in the center of the hut. "Sit. I will tell you a story. I have not always lived a hermit's life. Years ago, I lived at court in the employ of King Gav the Brave."

"My father!"

"I was one of his most trusted advisors, but I was not alone. Another had the king's other ear. Our counsels were never in harmony, and over the years, your father learned to heed my wisdom and the kingdom prospered.

"Still, the Dark Counselor remained. As the king had no heir, the counselor's desire was for the throne. He was waiting for an opportune time to take your father's life."

"He would kill the king?"

The old man eased down onto the floor. "He would do much more. When the news came that Queen Ele was expecting a child, the Dark Counselor's fury knew no bounds. Now there would be an heir. The kingdom would be out of reach for another generation."

The old man bowed his head. "I cannot tell you how close he came to destroying the queen and the child. Their protection consumed my every thought."

"I owe you a debt I cannot repay."

"Perhaps, but I did not foresee the depth of the counselor's treachery, the pain of which you now endure."

"What? Speak."

He inhaled deeply. "A child was born, a boy, handsome and perfect. But sadly, the child was stillborn. No breath of life filled his lungs."

"But, I have no dead brother."

"Quiet, sir. Your father ran the child into the court, lifted the boy to heaven, and prayed. Every court official and advisor gathered around the baby to lay hands on his tiny frame. Every advisor."

"Including the Dark Counselor?"

"I did not see him, cloaked as he was. We prayed a blessing on the child and the kingdom. And the baby coughed. The baby came to life. But the Dark Counselor had not joined in our blessing. Instead, he placed a curse."

A tingle ran down the White Knight's back. "But I was that child. King Gav, that's my father ... Pray tell, where did the Dark Counselor lay hold of me?"

The old man reached over and removed the knight's boot. He touched his foul toe. "Here." The man smiled. "He thought that you would quickly die. You did not."

The White Knight shuddered. "Who is this man? What is his name?"

"Get out of the car, Martin. I'm late to the library. You'll have to go to school today."

I blink and wipe sweat from my forehead. "Yeah. We're at school? Okay. "

Find the beginning. Find the Black Knight.

CHAPTER 17

I CHECK IN AT THE OFFICE, LEAN OVER THE COUNTER, and hand Ms. Corbitt a note.

"I saw a shrink. The man's brilliant. If you ever need advice, I'll set you up."

Ms. Corbitt glares. "I don't need a shrink, Martin."

"Never can be too sure. What's your first name?"

She yanks off her glasses and glares. "None of your business."

I lower my voice. "Two questions. Were you named after a relative? And is that relative dead?"

She looks pale, and I nod. "You might want to check into this guy. He's a death dude, but I think he's pretty good with curses too."

From inside his office Principal Creaker clears his throat. "I just spoke with the health teacher. He seems to think that you should be excused from detention to run on the track team."

"I totally forgot," I glance into his office. "That's today."

"I told him it would not be fair to release you and detain Ms. Snow for the same crime. So … the terms of your parole will dictate that Julia accompanies you each afternoon. She doesn't need to run, of course, but she does need to watch practices from the stands." He winks. "How do you feel about that?"

"She won't do it." I shake my head. "She's mad."

"Make her … unmad, son."

"Unmad?"

"Shoo." He whisks me out of the office.

Undo the curse. Unmad the girl.

There's still hope. Death said so.

I find Charley at lunch sitting with a herd of guys.

"Charley," I bump his back with my lunch bag. "I need your help."

"Oh, do you now? Kind of like I needed yours. How does it feel not to get it?"

I grab his collar and pull. His butt slides off the bench and onto the floor. He's up and in my face in a hurry.

"What's wrong with you?" He shoves my chest.

"This isn't a stupid story. This is life and death." I shove back.

Charley breathes deeply. "Life and death? Sure it is." Shove.

I nod. Shove back.

"Explain," he says, and shoves.

"I'm calling it Operation Save Martin. I've been talking to Dr. Death all morning and the man is a genius. He's from Boston, you know. He told me I needed to find the beginning. I think I'll need help."

Charley leans forward. "I have no idea what you're talking about." Big shove.

"Right." I grab his sleeve and yank him away from the table. "Meet me at the boxcar at midnight. The Barn Owl should be hibernating, Poole should be free, and I'm going to try and convince Julia."

His eyes widen. "Julia, or *your* Julia."

"Just Julia. I need a commitment here."

"*You* need to be committed here."

I wait.

"Fine. Tonight. Midnight. At the boxcar." His eyes narrow. "Better be life and death."

"Thanks." I slap his back hard. *That's one; now for Julia.*

I run toward the lunchroom doors.

"Hold on, young man."

It's Gladys, the head cook. I don't know why we call her Gladys. She's the only staff that we call by their first name. I don't even know if she has a second name. Maybe it's Gladys too. Gladys Gladys.

"Yeah?" I wince and peek into the hall, stuffed with kids. I don't have time for Gladys Gladys.

"Do you notice what we're having today?"

I shrug.

"Here's a hint. Small, round, purple, and staining. I don't know how Principal Creaker has allowed you to sail on without apologizing to the kids. But this seems the appropriate day."

She points to the loudspeaker, and I tramp over and pick up the cordless mic.

Gladys Gladys's arms fold over her apron. She is a large woman, imposing, and at times terrible. "Make this sincere." She flicks the mic switch to *on* and cranks the volume. Feedback squeals and everyone winces.

"Children. Martin Boyle would like to say something to you."

The group hushes. I scan the silent mob. Waiting. Wondering. What will Martin say? Any other year, I would snivel and grovel. But no, behold the Dandingo! I feel the power.

"Yeah, well, I — " I glance at Gladys Gladys and run to the other side of the lunchroom. "Has anyone seen Julia Snow?"

Hands shoot up.

Gladys pounds toward me, arms outstretched —
looking like my deployed airbag with legs. I keep moving. "Where is she now?"

"Check the gym!" A girl yells from table four.

"Give me ... give ... that mic, Martin!" Gladys loses
air fast.

I weave between tables. Kids pull in their feet for
me, cheer me as I go.

"And, uh," I gesture around the lunchroom. "I see
you all have prunes."

The kids groan. One long, loud groan.

Gladys Gladys pulls up, doubles over and huffs. She
peeks up from across the room.

"It's been brought to my attention that many of you
were purpled last time we had prunes, and you probably
got in trouble at home. I'm sorry for that whole thing.
It's just ..." I peek at a prune cup, reach down, and lift
it off a kid's plate. "These little buggers taste so bad." I
pluck a prune out of its purple bath. "And fly so good."
I fling it over the tables, over Gladys Gladys, toward the
garbage bins.

Swish!

"Viva la Martin!" Hector stands and whips his
prunes, and the room erupts.

I shouldn't have done it. I know it. But it felt so good.

I drop the mic and flee the carnage.

Next stop, gymnasium.

Two minutes later I burst into the gym. "Julia?"

I'm alone and my heart sinks. I quickly stroll to health class. I'm the first one to arrive. Laughing, purple kids stream in behind me. I stare at the announcement speaker hanging from the ceiling.

Five, four, three, two —

"Martin Boyle, to the lunchroom please. Martin Boyle."

I sit down across from Creaker and Gladys Gladys. I'm flanked by two custodians and surrounded by purple. Purple lights, purple windows, purple walls.

Nobody says a word.

I peek at the principal. "Do you know my mother?"

Another crease marks his forehead.

"Do you know what it's like to live thirteen years without doing anything? No frog collecting, no snake catching, no dirt digging, no fly swatting, no worm touching, no baseball playing, no Christmas tree cutting, no egg breaking, no cow milking, no pony riding, no fair going, no convertible riding, no snowball fighting ..." I breathe. "No lake swimming, ice-fishing, tree climbing, nothing. Do you know what thirteen years of that makes a kid want to do?"

He tongues the inside of his cheek and shakes his head.

"It makes you want to throw a prune. It makes you want to grab a stupid mic and run away from Gladys Gladys and fling a prune." I push my hand though my hair. "I know it wasn't right."

More silence. Creaker and Gladys Gladys exchange a glance and nod. Creaker stands. "Young man, I came in here to suspend you from school. I think, however, we'll go with Gladys's idea. Now if you'll excuse me, I have another prune flyer to prepare."

Gladys grins, then swallows it. She's trying to stay tough but it isn't working. "Bring out the tray!" Ms. Watershed rolls out the metal cart covered with prune cups. There must be twenty of them.

"Since you and prunes seem to have a natural affection for each other, why not get to know them even more intimately? Eat."

I frown and slowly palm a cup. Ms. Watershed hands me a fork. A minute later, I've downed three hideous prunes.

"And another."

I slowly reach for a cup and pause. "How many — "

"All."

"Twenty prune cups?"

"Twenty-eight. One for each table that is, once again, purple."

I slowly nod. And eat. At five, juice dribbles down my chin. At eleven, the stomach ache starts. I swallow the last four prunes with my head collapsed on the table.

Gladys Gladys smiles and pats my back. "Feel free to toss a prune anytime. Have a good day."

CHAPTER 18

I SPEND THE REST OF THE DAY IN THE NURSE'S OFFICE, shuffling back and forth from cot to bathroom. It gives me a lot of time to think. A lot of time to write.

Plenty of time to groan.

"The pain, sir. It increases each day." The White Knight stuffed his foot back into his boot. "But the Dark Counselor's interest in Alia. From where does that come?"

"Is it not clear? You lived. Your union with Alia places her in succession and your death will not give him the throne he desires. He must deal with both of you. And Alia is beautiful. The Dark Counselor is, after all, a man."

"A man now known as the Black Knight."

"Yes." The old man turned and stared out the window. "When he left your father's court he took many with him. They follow him out of fear, but follow they do. They gave him that name."

"But what is his true name? His name from birth?"

The old man winced. "The rest of the story you know. The Black Knight imprisoned Alia in the stone. Yet he was unaware that in doing so, he would not be able to free her. He never did believe in the prophecies. Thus, he needed one pure in heart. He needed you." The old man hobbled to the corner. "He needs you no longer."

The White Knight stared at the open door. "How do you come to know all these things? An old man, in a hut of mud — "

Then, behind him, a low growl. The knight slowly rose and turned.

"Not always an old man," Tas licked the fur on his arm.

The knight reached for his sword. "Your teeth, they sunk into my arm, they snapped my bone."

The jackal paced back and forth. "Did it not heal?"

The knight frowned and worked his arm. He had not noticed that pain was no more.

"Yes. How — "

"Sometimes ..." The jackal froze, "the one who breaks is also the one to heal. Had your arm not broken, you would not have traveled slowly. You would not have paused in the cave. You would not have been captured." Tas lay down. "You would not be here."

The White Knight slowly sheathed his sword and walked to the door. "So there is yet hope to find Alia?" A sharp pain stretched from his hip to his stomach. "Hope to live?"

He turned, and the old man smiled and closed his eyes. "There is always hope."

The final bell rings, and I haul my stomach cramps up to detention.

I collapse in a seat beside Julia and clutch my gut.

"Dying early?" She speaks into her lap and doesn't turn.

"Nope. But that's one of two things I want to talk to you about. This morning, I spoke with Death and — "

"Comforting."

"Not with death death. With Dr. Death. He's a … doesn't matter. In his office, I figured out how to break the curse."

"You did," Julia mutters.

"Now Dr. Death is brilliant. He's from Boston and he's like Death Einstein and … whatever, but the one who helped me the most was you."

"Me."

"That picture. The new one. I was looking at it while Death was talking about Irene and it hit — I just need to find the beginning, you know? Who is the Black Knight grabbing my toe? I need to find out where the curse started and undo it."

"Grabbing *your* toe?" She peeks at me. "You're the knight?"

I shrug and give a weak grin.

"And do you know anything about where it started?" she asks.

"No, but I know who the first Martin was. I know where he's lying right now. I think we can figure this out!"

"Martin? Julia? Please come here." Purse-lips gestures to me.

"So what do you say?" I whisper and stand. "Will you help?"

She stands and doesn't say anything.

"You don't look unmad yet. Listen, just be at the boxcar in my backyard at midnight."

"Martin! Julia!"

We reach the front and Purse-lips glances from Julia to me.

"I have a note signed by the principal and the health teacher. You are to be on the track right now."

I groan. "But my gut — "

"And you, young lady, are to be sitting on the bleachers."

Julia looks at me.

"That's the other thing. I kind of cut a deal for us." I nod toward the door. "I'll tell you on the way."

I stagger into the locker room, both hands clutching my abdomen. I thought I had ejected all the prunes, but a few must still be rattling around.

Coach has laid out my track uniform. I slowly strip and step into my shorts.

"No, no!" I dash to the toilet and empty out yet again. I exhale hard, grab my shirt and cleats, and push outside. I walk slowly across a field covered with dandelions. They're pretty, pretty like I've not noticed before. I bend over and pluck a bouquet.

Julia might like 'em.

"Over here, Martin!"

The track team sits in a clump around Coach. I check the stands. Julia sits in the middle toward the top.

So does Poole.

Boxcar boy smiles and waves and scoots closer to Julia. Opportunistic weasel.

"Here he is," Coach announces. "Gang, I want you to welcome Martin onto the team, our new hurdler."

The entire team stands and pats my back, shakes my hand. A bunch of their fingers are stained purple.

"Easy now," Coach breaks up the group. "Looks like fitting in won't be a problem." He points to the far side of the track. "I set up the hurdles over there. Had to dust them off." He laughs. Nobody else does, and Coach clears his throat. "I'd like to get a baseline of your hurdling ability. Head on over and show us what you've got."

Inside, a rumble, deep and ugly. "That's maybe not such a great idea today. I could stretch instead."

"Go on, Martin," David Hany calls out. "You jumped a table in the lunchroom. Show Coach."

A chorus chimes in, and I peek into the stands. Julia stares down at me. Poole waves.

Knights. Knights are loyal, generous, and brave. Chivalry and all that. Poole is definitely not a knight. Little sneak.

"Fine. I'll do it."

I stretch and saunter around the track to the hurdles. My audience watches from the distance, but I hear pieces:

"This kid can run."

"Flying through the lunchroom."

I close my eyes and see purple. That was before.

"Track. Why did I want to run track?" I walk up to the first hurdle. "Be nice to me. Duck a little, will ya? I'm fresh off a prune incident. Ever eaten prunes? Think of a toxic raisin on steroids."

The hurdle doesn't answer.

"Don't suppose you're familiar. But if you peek into the stands you'll see a girl and I'd really like —"

Why am I talking to a hurdle?

I back toward the start line, bend over like I've seen hurdlers bend.

Then I feel it. More bowel rumblings.

Crack!

From across the field, Coach fires a gun and I leap

forward, faster, faster toward the first hurdle. I slow up, plant my foot and soar ... smack into the stupid thing. I tumble forward and land hard on my rear.

Not now!

I tense and stand and race off the track toward the port-a-potty. Inside, I plop down and my guts explode. No time to be lazy. I finish and leap out toward the track and hurdle number two. Plant, soar, tumble. Stagger to the potty. Eight hurdles. Eight frantic flights toward the can.

Dumb prunes!

I stumble out dazed. The hurdles have been replaced. Poole stretches at the starting line.

"Supposed to go over them." He takes off, reaches the first, and leaps.

"Easy, see?"

Leap, leap, leap.

"Nothing to it." He waves at me as he crosses the finish line.

Claps and cheers erupt from my team.

"Hey, kid!" Coach runs toward Poole. "What's your name?"

"Oops, gotta go." Poole dashes over and slaps me on the back. "I hear there's a meeting tonight at my place."

"Yeah." I glance at Julia. She's standing and whoo-hooing and shouting. "Midnight."

Poole scampers over the fence surrounding the track and disappears.

Coach huffs up to me. I peek at him.

"How'd I do?"

"Hideous." He gasps for air. "Who ... who was that kid?"

"He doesn't go here. You won't see him again." Julia still goes nuts. "I promise."

CHAPTER
19

THE NIGHT IS COOL, AND I TIPTOE OUT OF THE HOUSE with my arms full. Computer, projector, white sheet. My belly cramps, reminders of where I've spent most of my day, slow me to a stroll. Ahead of me, flashlight beams criss-cross inside the boxcar.

I hoist the load inside and climb up.

Poole's gone all out. There's a ratty couch, an old La-Z-Boy, a small end table, and a lamp that looks very much like the one from Dad's study, but now's not the time for questions.

"What'd you do to your shirt?" Charley walks toward me and shines his beam on my chest.

"Permanent marker. It's a coat of arms. Knights used to have them." I touch my chest. "I needed a good symbol."

"And you chose purple rocks?"

"Prunes, Charlie. Those are prunes."

"Lights out, guys," Poole says, and flashlight beams go dark. Click. He turns on the lamp, and the boxcar fills with a hazy glow.

"What do you think, Marty?"

I smirk at Julia on the couch, nod to Charley, who sits on the chair. "Nice. Very nice."

Poole points at a toilet seat in the corner. "I dug up a special seat just for you."

"You're getting funnier by the day." I set the computer and the projector on the table, plug in, and with Charley's help, hang the sheet with duct tape.

"I want to thank you all for being here. What we discuss stays between us in what I've dubbed *Operation Save Martin*."

"Operation Save Martin." Poole collapses on the couch by Julia. "I like it. O. S. M. Otters Swim ... Magnificently."

"Orangutans Swing Marvelously," says Julia.

"Oh, Stupid Margarine," Charley blurts. He's a golden lab dying for attention. We roll our eyes and turn toward him.

"Get it?" he continues. "O stands for Oh. S stands for Stupid ..." Charley's voice trails away.

"Yes, S is for Stupid. We all have our gifts." I kneel and set up the PowerPoint presentation, and soon the computer screen shines off the sheet. "I want to go over where we've been before assigning duties. Slide one."

Julia clicks the screen and an image appears.

"At a very gruesome ceremony, Martin discovers his name is cursed and he has three months to live. This figure has now been downgraded to less than two, depending on when Aunt Jenny delivers. Slide two."

"Poole and Julia appear. This means that we have three believers in the curse. This increases the likelihood of mission success three-fold. If Charley gets it, we'll have four. Slide three."

"Gets what?" Charley throws up his hands. "What am I supposed to get?"

Poole points at me. "Marty here is going to be dead in a couple months because his name is cursed. Following?"

Charley frowns at me. "Oh. Yeah. That makes sense." Poor kid looks lost.

I continue. "Definition of success. Martin lives beyond the point of the new Martin's birth. Are we clear so far?"

Julia nods. Poole points at the sheet. "Very good presentation, Marty."

"Wait! You're dying?" says Charley. "You never told —"

I clear my throat. "We go on. Enter Dr. Death, a death expert from Boston —"

Poole taps Julia and whispers, "Ever been to Boston? It is beautiful in —"

"Shh!" Her gaze is glued to me. "Go on, Martin."

"The way to undo a curse is to go to the root, the beginning, and undo it."

"Words have power." Poole folds his arms. "Been telling him this all along."

"Next slide. This is a photo of the cemetery. And this is the headstone of the first Martin Boyle buried there. It can be conjectured that he may be close to the beginning, and therefore connected to the curse."

I give a shallow cough and breathe in, only no air enters. I swallow hard and gasp. A whisper of oxygen fights through.

"Great work, Marty." Poole straightens and leans forward. "Give me an assignment."

"Hold on." I grab the side of the boxcar. I feel unsteady, nervous. Then as quickly as it comes, the sensation goes.

Julia licks her lips. "You okay?"

I give a quick nod. "Finally then, it comes to this." I flick the next slide, one of me standing near a port-a-potty. "Martin Boyle will focus on specific information about the first Martin in the cemetery. Dad has info, but asking him lands me on shrinks' couches, and I don't have the time, so I'll need to figure this out firsthand."

Click. Julia sitting on the bleachers. "Julia will gather all the info she can about ancient curses. Who made them? Were there any famous ones? Did anybody live through them, etcetera." I gesture at her with my pointer. "Look for patterns. You need to become a curse expert."

"I'll do it."

"Julia? Next picture?"

"Oh, right." She clicks the screen and Poole appears, sleeping on his bench.

"When did you . . . ?"

I smile and turn to Poole. "And you. The first Martin was in this area hundreds of years ago. I know little about him, but where he lived might matter. Can you figure out the fastest train routes across the city so that wherever his trail leads, we can follow?"

"You want me to map every train route that leaves my depot? And maybe get times and schedules?" He jumps and pumps a fist. "Right up my alley. I know just where to start. I'll ride the line a few times, just to be — "

"That's nice, Poole."

"What about me?" asks Charley. "Maybe I should work with Julia on the curse part."

Click. A picture of Charley superimposed on a wiener and lying in a bun.

Julia breaks out laughing and Charley jumps up. "How did you?"

"Photoshop. Now while the three of us sneak all over, we'll need cover. We'll need an excuse, a place to be. This will be our line: We're going to Charley's house. You need to stay home so it's believable."

"You want me to do nothing?"

I nudge his knee with my shoe. "Like a wiener in a bun. Just lie there."

Charley frowns. "It doesn't sound too important."

"That's probably the most important job," Poole nods soberly.

"Oh yes," Julia's eyes sparkle. "Absolutely."

Charley glances at her. "I guess then I'm the right guy for it. I won't let you down." He looks around. "None of you. Count on me to do … nothing?"

"We will." I flick off the projector. "Any questions?"

It's silent.

Poole rises and grabs a piece of sidewalk chalk from a bucket in the corner. "There." He makes a green tally on the boxcar's wall. "We're keeping track of passing days right here."

"Fine then." I swallow hard. "And one last thing."

I step in front of the light. "I've never been really athletic."

"You can say that again," Poole says. "Charley, you should have seen this guy today."

"I was admitting I've never been in good shape. That needs to change. What if the curse only affects sickly, skinny Martins? I need to be in great shape. I'll need your help."

My friends crowd around and we grasp hands. I reach for Julia's and feel a lump in her fist. She presses a hard object into my palm.

"My dad loved chess," she whispers. "I never really learned. But if you're a knight, you'll need a horse, right?"

I stare down at the chess piece, a beautifully carved white knight, the head of the horse fierce and proud.

"Yeah, I will." I look around the circle. "Although we'll be in touch, let's plan on meeting here in a few weeks — after we've examined evidence. Same time, same place. Hopefully, Operation Save Martin will be a success."

"OSM. OSM," Poole begins a whispered chant, and we all join in. "OSM. OSM."

"Why are we saying this?" Charley asks.

Poole shrugs. "Maybe this chant will break the curse."

"OSM? Oh, Stupid Me."

I exhale hard. *Okay, God. We're going to need a lot of help.*

Who was Martin Boyle? The first Martin Boyle?

I stare at Poole's tally wall, covered in green, yellow, and pink. I reach into the bucket.

"Blue, blue. I'm feeling blue … Get off there."

I gently remove a centipede from the chalk stick and add the thirty-eighth mark.

Thirty-eight days, one hour, and twenty-one — no twenty-two minutes — have passed since our boxcar meeting, and I'm no closer to an answer than I was weeks ago.

How do you find out about a dead man?

I gaze around the boxcar. The night is quiet, except for the distant sound of frogs.

Would have liked some company tonight. Poole, you must be out foraging.

I shuffle inside the house. I wander into Dad's office and pull *The White Knight* out from the bottom drawer. I lift my feet onto Dad's desk and doodle in the margins. I can't sleep. Early-morning and late-night runs with Poole leave me so full of energy, there's almost no need. Coach calls me the most improved freak of running nature he's ever seen. How cruel to feel so strong right before the end.

The White Knight rode through the night, pausing when his steed grew tired. Standing beneath the starry night, he breathed deep for the first time in many moons. But the air stuck in his throat and his stomach turned. Somewhere out there was Alia.

He journeyed forward, over hill, through forest, and into the desert. Hope of finding his lost love grew dim.

"Perhaps, Sir Knight, she also looks for you."

"Who goes there?" The knight spun around. "Show your-self, coward!"

"Down here, sir."

The knight sheathed his sword, dropped to his knees, then lowered himself further onto his belly. There he was, face-to-face with a centipede.

"You, dear sir, are a centi—"

"I know what I am, and I also know who you seek."

"But how?"

The centipede slowly turned and gestured with thirty legs. "Do you see that imprint in the sand?"

"Aye."

"I had this same conversation one day ago with a fair maiden."

"Alia!" The White Knight crawled to her impression. It was her. He could feel it.

He grabbed the bug by a leg and lifted him to nose level. "Where did she go?"

"She looks for you, sir." The bug twirled slowly in the air. "If you'd kindly set me down—"

The knight did. "And where does she look?"

The bug brushed himself off and saluted. "I told her to return to the spot you found her last."

"Horrors! That would be the dungeon. The dungeon be-neath the magic fortress."

I slam the notebook closed. The magic fortress. The residence of the Black Knight. And the one place that, according to both Dad and Google, the first Martin has been. If I want to find the beginning ...

To the fort.

I rise and light-foot toward the basement door, reach it, and silently descend.

Underwear World is accurately named — briefs ball-up everywhere, and socks are strewn across the floor. Dad's fast asleep on the La-Z-Boy, his nineteenth-century rifle across his lap. And in the corner, resting on the table, his Fort Snelling uniform, buttons shined and ready to go.

I creep up to him. He cracks open an eyelid and I jump.

"Never sneak up on a man with a gun." He straightens his chair.

I clear my throat. "But — "

"Sentries never sleep." Dad stretches, cracks his knuckles. "How is the story going up there?"

"You know about that too?"

Dad sets his gun down beside the chair. "I do." He cocks his head. "Over the past month or two, you've been doing some changing. Some growing. I've been watching closely. Julia. The running team. Even detention. You're living, son."

I swallow hard. "It's harder than I thought. It's been a strange few months …" I swipe underwear onto the floor and plop onto the couch. I try to speak, but words don't come. Dad squints and strokes his chin.

"Go on. What is it?"

"I've never asked you before, but … would you ever take me to work? Not just to see the place, but to, you know, stay there with you for a whole reenactment? Three or four days or whatever?"

Dad's hand freezes. "Say that again."

"I asked if you would ever take — "

"Oh, I heard you the first time." He rubs his palms together. "Now we're talking. I've been waiting for this moment!" Dad flies from the chair, scurries to the closet, and pulls out a tiny blue uniform. He walks it back to me and holds it up to my chest. "A small man's uniform just right for my big man!"

I stroke the front of it. "I take it that's a yes. Would you mind if we brought someone along? Well, if I can find him?"

"Sorry, son. We don't have time for late-night permissions."

I nod. "This kid comes with his own permissions. He's, well, kind of a vagrant."

"Vagrant, huh?" Dad eases back into his chair. "Is he local?"

"Very."

"And you've know him for …"

"A couple months. I even had him over when you were gone."

Dad nods. "Well, if he's been to the house and passed the Elaina test, I don't see a problem." He smiles. "Get some sleep, sentry. We'll leave in four hours."

I lay back. It's been years since I've been down here. Years since I've felt close to Dad. It feels too good to lose him now.

CHAPTER 20

"Poole! Wake up!"

I shake his carcass. I have no idea how rocks sleep, but I better understand the phrase.

"Poole!" I kick his legs hard. He doesn't flinch.

"Poole!" I punch his shoulder. "Fool!" Punch. "Drool!" Punch. "Poole!"

He rolls over, eyes wide open, and leaps to his feet. "Mornin' Marty." He stretches and shakes his head hard. "What's going on?" Two seconds from out cold to wide awake. Freaky. He walks a circle around me, reaches out and tugs at a button. "The Civil War ended, you know."

I clutch his forearm and drag him out of the boxcar. "We have work to do. You're coming with me and Dad to Fort Snelling." I face him square. "This is some serious first Martin research. I might need help."

"Think Julia might be helpful—"

"No, she wouldn't."

"Just asking, is all."

We meet Dad, the soldier, next to the Suburban. He whistles and pitches weapons through the hatch. He pauses, bayonet out, and stares at Poole. Poole stares back at Dad. This is brutal — it's a stare-off.

Dad slowly reaches out his hand. "Who do we have here?"

"Name's Poole."

"Is that first or last?"

"Sorta both." They still vice grip each other with their gazes.

I slap my hands over both their faces. "Break it up."

"So be it." Dad shakes my hand free. "You have a good, tough stare. I like that in a kid." He glances from Poole to me and back again. "My son tells me we don't need to check with any parents before …"

Poole blinks watery eyes — I reckon from the stare-off — and shakes his head. Dad tousles his hair. "A rug like this, you'll fit right in." He winks. "I don't have a uniform for you, but I reckon I can scrounge up something at the fort." Dad grabs Poole's shoulder. "So long as you don't mind fighting on our side."

The 5:00 a.m. ride is quiet and lulls me to sleep. I wake to pebbles clinking against our underbelly, and we pull into the Fort Snelling lot.

"Up, soldiers." Dad slaps my knee. "It's time to go inside. You'll meet the rest of the Fifth Regiment."

I groan and push out and take one step toward the fort. My stomach aches and my head spins. I grab for Poole's shoulder.

"Hang on to me. I think I'm going to — Whoa."

Both legs buckle. Poole wraps his arm under my shoulder and lowers me back into the car. "Sit here, friend. It just hit ya?"

I swallow hard and swipe sweat off my forehead. I'm clammy. The curse.

Dad laughs with a clump of soldiers near the fort's gate. Poole swallows hard. "Is this sick the same sick as the sick at the cemetery?"

"I think so."

He rubs his chin. "We might be getting close. Can you stand?"

I rise slowly and the world steadies. Poole pats my back. "Onward soldier."

We join Dad beneath the Gatehouse.

"Gentlemen," Dad eyes me and straightens. "I'd like to introduce you to Privates Boyle and Poole, fresh up from — where did you two say you were from?"

I peek at Poole. He smiles confidently. "St. Paul. Fresh up from St. Paul."

A fat soldier spits a wad that splats over my shoe. "Ain't never heard of it. Lad's had a touch of the scurvy."

1820. We're in 1820.

I slap Poole. "What my friend meant to say is St. Louis."

"Home." The fat guy smiles and nods. "Heard talk that the First Regiment is coming up to spell us. That true, Boyle?"

Dad bumps my foot with his rifle butt.

"Uh, yeah. There's talk. You might be heading home soon."

"Hallelujah! Private Scuttle at your service." A slim soldier reaches out his hand. "I don't think I could bear the privations of another winter up here. It's not possible —"

"What do you know of privations, Scuttle? You spent the cold snap feigning sickness and heating your backside in front of a fireplace." The big man turns to me. "Private Cork. Pleased to meet you. Any relation to Martin Boyle — *the* Martin Boyle?"

Dad jumps in. "A naming coincidence. He and Poole are new recruits. The first reverie is in five minutes, and if Colonel Snelling sees Poole out of uniform, he'll be cat-whipped for sure. Scuttle?"

"Yes, sir. I'll get him an army issue." He grabs Poole. "Can you run? You don't want to make a bad impression on the Colonel."

They hustle beneath the Gatehouse arch and into the fort.

"Let's go, men." Dad leads us into the central clearing, where sleepy soldiers and musicians with drum and bugle mill about.

I grab Dad and pull him to the side. "This pretending is great and all. But I was wondering if there was someone around who could give me a tour and answer questions and stuff."

The look he gives me is grim and terrible. "You didn't travel seven hundred miles up the Mississippi to take a tour. Your mother and fiancée —"

Fiancée?

"Aren't you pushing this fantasy a little too far?"

"Perhaps you *were* touched with the scurvy. The missive I received from Julia was clear. She wants to see you back safely in a few years. She was none too pleased when you enlisted, remember that." He straightens my buttons. "Sharpen up, soldier. Or you'll find yourself in the Guard House."

I smile. Fiancée. Julia. Okay, I'll go along with this for a while.

Fifes tweet and bugles blast around me.

Dad yanks me back to the stone barracks. "Roll call. Look sharp."

I don't feel sharp. I feel dull. Very dull.

A fine-dressed man strides out from the only house within fort walls. Clad in a clean, blue uniform with shiny buttons, the soldier struts like Mr. Halden, as though men should cower before him. They do. He slows when he reaches the hundred soldiers gathered on our side of the parade grounds. Beside him, a weasely man with a nasal voice:

"Arrington."

"Here."

"Artle."

"Aye."

"Bain."

"Present."

"Boyle."

"We're." My *what* and Dad's *here* combine and the regiment chuckles.

"Silence. Boyle step forward."

Dad takes two giant steps forward. I peek around the head in front of me.

"Officer Boyle. Are you mocking the calling of the roll?"

"No, sir!" Dad shouts.

"Your display caused a disruption. For that, you will be given —"

"Hang on." I step out and slowly weave between rows of men. "Are you Colonel Snelling?"

More laughter.

"Speak one more time at your peril, soldier."

I raise my hands toward the sky. "But I just got here and I didn't get the official rulebook, you know, like when Halden gave me The Treatment. Hot shower, cold shower, like that. I didn't get the rules. And I don't want Da — this officer to get in trouble when it should be me. My bad."

It's silent throughout the fort.

Snelling clears his throat. "Do you realize that insubordination leads to mutiny?"

"No, sir. I mean, yes, sir. You've helped me see the error of my ways."

"Meet me in my quarters at noon."

"Sure. I mean, yes, sir. Where are your quarters?" I scan the yard, point at the only two-story home in sight. "In there?"

Laughter explodes from the men, and a lone voice calls, "He's a jester from St. Louis!"

"We'll see if he still jests after our visit." Colonel Nasty backhands the Weasel. "Continue the call!"

"Bronson."

"Here!"

They finish roll and Snelling leaves and men exhale. They gather around me and pat me on the back.

"I've been wanting to speak at ease during the call ever since I got here," Scuttle salutes me. "Boyle, you're a man after your own name." He turns smartly and disappears into the barracks.

"Hey! What does that mean? What do you know about my name?"

"Martin," Dad pulls me aside, whispers, "You shouldn't have done that."

"But I screwed up. I'll take the punishment." I point over my shoulder. "What did that guy mean 'A man after your own name'?"

Dad exhales. "We'll go talk to the Colonel. He'll understand that you're just here for fun and you're not a recruit."

I press my hand against his forehead. "Sir, you seem to have a touch of fever. I did too before I left my Julia in St. Louis. A poultice of fig juice seemed to do the trick."

Dad removes his cap and rubs his forehead. "Private Boyle. As you were."

CHAPTER 21

I SIT OUTSIDE THE FORT'S GENERAL STORE — THE ONE marked Luther Leonard, Sutler — watching soldiers and women shuffle in and out.

"Psst."

I lean forward and peer around. The sound came from nowhere, and I gentle back against cold wood.

"Psst yourself." I fold my hands. "If this is some wacko curse-related voice in my head, I'm a little busy right now."

"Psst. Kid."

The voice rises from beneath me, and I stand and kick my talking stool.

"Ouch! Never seen a bench speak before?"

A young boy, maybe eight, leaps out of a nearby rain barrel and plops down on my stool. "Did you like that? Did you know there are tunnels? Everywhere. Beneath all the buildings. Most of the men don't know 'em, but I do."

I retake my seat. "I'm Private Boyle. And you are?"

"Squirrel. Call me Squirrel." He looks me all over. "You look like a kid."

"Am not. I'm engaged, you know."

"I don't believe you."

"Am too. Her name is Julia."

"Let's see your ring."

I stretch my bare fingers. "Lost it. It was bitter cold, and fortunately I came across the teepee of friendly Indians. I traded the ring for food."

He wipes his sweaty hair from his eyes. "Wise move. Do you want to take a look around? Since you're new here and all."

"That would be good." I grimace. "I have a few hours to kill. The Officer of the Day —"

"Officer Fennel."

"Yeah," I say, "him. He's trying to decide whether I should be allowed to start sentry duty. I guess I caused quite a disturbance when I arrived. Wait."

Thankful. I haven't erupted yet today.

"I'm having trouble thinking — Got it. I'm thankful for this squirrel that crawled out from beneath my bench!"

"Quiet down!" he hisses. "It's best not to let everyone know where you are."

I whisper, "Fair enough. Lead on."

Squirrel shows me the barracks and the guard towers. He introduces me to everyone in the commissary and shows me how to work the well.

"One last place you should see."

He leads me to a stone building. I know what it is, iron bars are a giveaway. "The Guard House. There's a Reprobate in there. That's the reason for the guard."

"I don't need to see inside." I turn.

"Okay, I'll get back to my tutor." Squirrel skips away. "I just thought that being a Boyle, you might want to talk to him about Martin."

I freeze. "Come back!"

Squirrel is gone.

My heartbeat quickens and I breathe deeply. *Calm down, Martin.* I approach the guard. "I hear you have a Reprobate."

"A drunkard." The guard turns his head and spits. "You know how the Colonel feels about drunkards."

"Absolutely." I bite my lip. "Mind if I step inside?"

"Go on in." Spit, spit. "Don't speak to him. He's to be isolated for another twenty-four hours."

I slip inside the darkened building. It takes my eyes time to adjust, and when they do, there's not much to see. A table, a bench, and a thick wooden door with iron bars. I step forward and peek through the door. Inside are two solitary confinement rooms and a third enclosure with a mattress and a sleeping man.

"Excuse me," I whisper. "Mr. Reprobate, sir?"

He doesn't shift.

"Um, hmm!" My throat does nothing either. I lower myself onto the long bench outside the cell area. Cast-iron keys hang above my head.

This is dumb. What am I thinking? Like some snoozing actor is gonna know anything about two hundred years ago. Go to the origin of the curse? Thanks for nothing, Dr. Death. You have a nice office and nice plants and a nice secretary and lots of years ahead, but I have a little over a week, and I'm feeling dizzy for no reason and I'm only thirteen.

"I'm running out of time to search — "

"Who you looking for?" The Reprobate rolls over and groans. "What day is it?"

"Uh, I don't even know what year it is. Oops, I'm not supposed to talk to you."

He winces and swings his legs over the edge of the bed. "I don't deserve to be in here. I didn't do anything uncomely." He pushes his hands through his hair. "I just wanted to forget."

I peek toward the door and lean in. "Forget what?"

He shakes his head and buries it in his hands.

"I know how that feels." I stand. "Well, I gotta get going. It's almost noon. Nice to meet you." I shoot him an awkward wave. "I'll be around when you get out, so in case I bump into you, my name's Boyle. Martin Boyle."

The Reprobate hurtles himself against the bars and

reaches for my coat. "Martin, is that you?" He wipes his eyes. "I knew you looked familiar … But I saw you buried! I dug the hole myself. How — " His eyes narrow and he whispers, "How?"

I yank free, trip over the spit can, and fall on my butt. The guard rushes in.

"What did our Reprobate do to you?"

"Nothing," I say. "He did nothing."

"Do you have amnesia, Martin?" The prisoner strains his arm through the bars. "It's me, James. James Delaney, the stonemason. Your neighbor! You saved my family. You saved the entire camp. Don't you remember me?"

The guard rounds my shoulder with his arm and leads me outside. "I apologize. Poor man suffers from fits." He leads me outside, but James's voice rises to a holler. "It was my hand on the stone. I chiseled it last winter; I would do it again for you. There can only be one Martin!"

A knife-like pain jabs my leg. I spin slowly and stare at the entrance. *Dad's words. Each year at the cemetery. Those are always Dad's words.*

"I need to go back in there!" I yank free, but the guard blocks my way.

"Calm, man. Do you not understand isolation?"

"Do you not understand *curse*?" I feint to the left, feint to the right, and leap toward the door and a screaming James.

The guard swings his musket, catches my foot, and I tumble to the ground. "You've just earned yourself a trip to the Colonel." He yanks me by the sleeve. "Howard!" Another soldier comes running. "Take my post!"

We stagger across the parade grounds. With each step I move farther from someone who knows something I desperately need to hear. Ahead is the nicest looking building in the whole place. The house. The Commanding Officer's Quarters. A distant bugle blows — the 12:00 p.m. call.

Noon. Right on time.

I'm whisked inside the brick building. It feels modern; at least it probably was in 1820. It kind of looks like our house, which feels years away.

Inside, kids laugh and race around. One scampers up to me.

"Squirrel? You live here? You're the Colonel's son?"

He grins. "Daddy." Squirrel peeks nervously into the back room. "I'm supposed to keep my distance from you."

"Why?" I ask.

"Josiah? Away from that man."

"Yes, Father." Squirrel turns and runs outside. I think to follow him, but three soldiers posted inside the doorframe change my mind.

"Come, Private." Colonel Snelling motions toward the back room. I follow him in and he closes the door behind us. Inside are a desk, two chairs, and a floor-to-ceiling post.

He shoots me a Creaker-look, eases down behind the desk, and lights a pipe. "Private Boyle ... with such a name." He blows a perfect smoke ring. "You know the standard events of this residence. To welcome strangers to the fort, for balls, for celebrations."

I straighten. "That sounds fun!"

He tongues his cheek. "None of these constitute why I've brought you here. You cannot plead ignorance to the riotous behavior you've caused."

"You call a few chuckles riotous? It's a good thing you don't serve prunes — "

"Silence!"

"Right," I whisper. "Not another word."

"You will find me a fair man, but a harsh one. When a soldier under my authority sparks discord, I act quickly. It is a cancer that must be dealt with immediately."

I say nothing.

"Good, you just took the first steps toward civility by holding your tongue. The cat should finish your journey."

"The cat?"

He strides to the door. "Steward!"

The Colonel turns back to me. "Remove your shirt and lean against the pole."

"You're kidding. Wait. This is enough. You're not Colonel Snelling, and I'm not Martin Boyle — well, okay, I'm Martin Boyle — but you're not Snelling. Your name is probably Leonard or Harry or something and your wife is Tina and you live in downtown Minneapolis. I'm not stripping for — "

"Strip!"

"Okay, okay." I slip out of my shirt. "Why am I doing this?"

"Nine lashes with the knotted rope should thrash the insubordination out of you." He turns toward the open door. "Steward!"

"Sorry, I was havin' trouble finding the cat."

Poole walks in and winks.

I stare. "How did — "

"How many lashes, sir?"

"Nine." Colonel Snelling puffs out one more blast of smoke. "Then show Private Boyle out." The Colonel exits the room, shutting the door behind him.

I stare at Poole. "How did you get this job?"

"You didn't bring me along for nothing. Now lean against the pole."

"You're not using that on me!" I back toward the wall.

Poole drops his arms and his volume. "'Course not. But in case the Colonel steps in ...'"

"Oh, good idea." I wrap my arms round the pole. Poole steps behind me.

"One!" Poole yells.

"Oh, stop, I can take no more!" I smile and give my most pitiful howl.

"Two!"

"The pain, the pain!"

We fake the beating, and I pretend to holler in agony.

"Nine!"

Whack! The knotted rope rips across my back and I fall forward.

"Oh!" I stumble up, my back on fire. "Why did you hit me?" I hiss.

"He might check your back. It should be welted a little. I had to give you one —"

The door flies open and Snelling stands in the entry. "Steward, you may leave. From the looks of it, our young Private Boyle will cause no more problems. Private Boyle, report to sentry duty at the Half Moon Battery." Poole leaves. I slip into my shirt and stumble outside. I don't know where I'm headed, I just need to be out of there; where my friend whips me because some guy named Leonard pretending to be Colonel Snelling tells him to.

"Half Moon. Half Moon." I peek back toward the Guard House where James sits behind bars. "I'll be back."

I run up the limestone steps to the top of the battery and my jaw drops. It's a stony platform that overlooks two huge rivers. I walk to the edge.

"One hundred feet down." A voice squeaks behind me. "That there's the Mississippi, and over there's the Minnesota. They come together beneath your feet. There's no more important watch than this." The sentry on duty walks up to me and extends a hand. "Private Powell. Pleased to make your acquaintance."

I shake his hand. "My name's Martin Boyle, uh, Private Boyle."

"Funny." He rolls his eyes, then squints hard and looks at me. "You're aren't jesting."

"No, that's me."

"Well, all right then, Boyle. You should know your way around." He frowns. "Where's your rifle?"

"I don't have one."

"Here." Powell hands me his. "Take mine. I'd be honored."

I slowly reach for the gun. "Is it ... loaded?"

"Of course. Ever shot a hostile Indian with a blank?"

I shake my head. *Mom would freak. Absolutely freak.*

"And one more thing. What am I watching for?"

"Anything." He points a pretend rifle over the edge. "Indians!" He runs to the other side of the battery and takes aim at the invisible enemy. "British!" Powell drops to his knees, whips his torso around and shoots. "French."

"Right." I turn toward the rivers, and my vision starts to blur. I swallow and lean hard on the rifle.

Powell descends the stairs behind me. "It really is an honor to have you here."

The wind whips over the top of the battery, and I sit down as dizziness returns. This may all be pretend, but it's the realest pretend I've ever known. In time, my legs feel strong enough to support, and I stand and watch mighty rivers converge. In the distance, a speedboat skips over the waves, coming closer, closer.

"Sentry Boyle spots danger! He rises to his feet. The threat approaches, fast, furious. It's a speedboat filled with hostile Indians. Boyle must think fast if he is to save the fort. He grabs the loaded gun, realizes not even the crackpots in this fort would give him a loaded weapon, takes aim at the boat, and fires—"

Kaboom!

I fall back on my butt as smoke rises from the barrel of the gun. *Oh no.* I scramble to the edge on my knees.

Whew! The boat zips on by and I crumble, face against limestone. Soldiers and questions surround.

"Who were you shooting at?"

"What did you see?"

"What are you thinking, man?"

Strong arms help me, noodly Private Boyle, down the steps and to Colonel Snelling's quarters.

The Colonel steps onto the porch and shakes his head. "Two days."

"Don't I get a trial? A phone call? Maybe a lawyer!" I run out of stupid television comments and armed guards shove me across the courtyard.

"Where am I going? What does two days mean?"

Guard House, straight ahead.

Inside my heart leaps. It's where I need to go. Nothing could be better. I walk back through the doorway on my own power and stop. "Where's James? The stonemason, where did he go?"

Spitter doesn't turn. He turns the key on the cell door and throws it open. "Went mad. The doctor said he suffers from deep confusion. We sent him home not one hour ago."

I grab for his uniform, but my escorts are quick and toss me into my new home. "I need to see him. See, my name is cursed and he knew something. I don't know what, but he chiseled something."

"Aye. The cornerstone of this very fort. In Colonel Snelling's residence. But you won't be seeing him anytime soon. As we speak, he's on a boat to St. Louis."

No, he's not! He's just a guy. A regular twenty-first century guy! He's probably stuck in traffic right now, so call his cell.

All three men spit tobacco at the pot and jostle outside. I stagger back to the wooden bed and lie down. It's hard and cool and damp, but it doesn't matter. Nothing matters. I was an hour away from finding out something. From talking to Martin's fake neighbor. Now it's over.

CHAPTER 22

A BUGLE WAKES ME FROM MY SLEEP, AND I THROW off my burlap blanket. I'm shivering, my neck hurts from sleeping in a feed trough, and there's a nailhead indent in the small of my back.

I reach in my pocket and remove Julia's chess piece. I turn it over in my fingers.

"I'm thankful for ... I'm thankful for ..." I follow a drip of water across a ceiling beam. It grows, wiggles, then splats onto my forehead.

"Nothing. I am officially not thankful anymore. God, I am tired of being whipped and thrown in jail by a man named Leonard. I'm tired of this crazy place. I'm tired of being alone and I'm sick of "dyink" and I don't want to kick the bucket and leave Poole and Charley fighting over the girl I like!"

"That was the most pathetic thankful yell I've ever heard."

Poole creeps in. "The guard won't be at roll call long, so I can't stay."

"Fine, fine. Don't stay. Enjoy your mattress—"

"Actually, I'm on a feather bed."

"Whatever! Go nap on your feather bed and eat your custard pies or whatever they serve—"

"Wild blueberry—"

"Wild blueberry pies and then enjoy your grimy years with Julia." I lie back down on the nail head, wince, and turn away from my friend.

It's quiet a long time. I hear shuffling feet. *He must have left.*

I half-roll and peek over my shoulder. Poole is digging his toe in the dirt. "Nothing's going to be the same without you."

I don't want to cry. Soldiers don't cry. Even dying ones. They lie there on the battlefield and close their eyes all tough-like. I feel a tear and whisper, "Miss you too."

I clear my throat. "You better get back to Leonard in the Officers' Quart—"

I jump up. "I'm thankful you are such a con artist!"

Poole cocks his head.

"I don't how you got into Snelling's quarters, but I need you to poke around for the cornerstone. It's in the Officers' Quarters. Can you do that?"

"Why am I doing that?"

"James knew me, or he knew the first me, or he

thought I was the first me — oh, it doesn't matter. He said 'There can only be one Martin,' just like Dad says every year. He said he chiseled my name in a stone, the cornerstone of this fort. You always say words have power. Doesn't that just reek of curseness?"

Poole's eyes grow wide. "I'm on it. You wait here."

"Funny, Poole."

He's gone for half the day.

"Blueberry pie," I mumble. "Feather beds and blueberry pie." I munch on my stale bread and dried beef. Finally I hear Poole talking to the guard. A moment later he pokes his head in.

"Found your cornerstone. There's nothing." He pulls out a scrap of paper. "Two names are carved in it: your friend James Delaney and William Goddard. Then there's a symbol, nothing I recognize. No mention of you. If there was more, it's gone now."

I exhale hard. "Maybe James was crazy."

Outside, the guard stands and salutes. Dad walks in, grabs the keys, and opens the cell door.

"Colonel Snelling has granted my request for time off. I thought I'd explore outside the fort." He gestures to me and I walk out, slow and stiff.

"I told him I'd like to hunt." Dad looks at Poole, then back to me. "I said I'd need a few men to accompany me, in case of Indian encounter. He said I could choose my companions." Dad puts his hand on my shoulder. "I choose you two." He leans over. "Let's go home, son."

The three of us walk across the parade grounds and beneath the Gatehouse arch. A soldier at the entrance offers Dad one final salute, and we step out to freedom.

"That was awesome!" Poole says. "Incredible! Melt-in-the-mouth-turkey, pudding — I'm talking three different kinds — and potatoes? With butter, with gravy, with stuffing ... and my room? You will not believe it. You won't. Ask me about it. See you can't, because you know you won't!"

I can't say anything. Dad can't either. I have no idea what he's thinking. Did I embarrass him? I didn't mean to.

We step into the Suburban and turn onto the highway. The present feels strange. Cars, loud horns, the Minneapolis/St. Paul airport. I look at my uniform. I don't feel like I belong here anymore. I don't feel like I belong anywhere.

"My first track meet is tomorrow at 4:00. I didn't think I'd be back in time, but Dad got me out of jail and my whipping should heal by then."

Mom's jaws tighten.

"Whipping? Did you say whipping?" Her gaze shifts to Dad. "Gavin. He said whipping. Explain this now."

Dad pushes his hand through his hair and shuffles toward Underwear World. He says nothing. I can't bear not knowing what he thinks.

Mom jumps in front of Dad's basement door, and the Owl spreads her wings.

Dad sighs heavy. "Yes, Elaina?"

"We did not discuss Martin's absence," she hisses.

"I left a note so you wouldn't worry."

Mom looks over his shoulder at my tattered, foul uniform — an up-and-down, horrified look. "He is dirty, slimy, and grungy. He is teeming with microbes. I smell them. He was beaten? He was jailed? Good gracious, Gavin! What are you doing to our child?"

Dad lifts his gaze from the ground and turns. He puts both his hands on my shoulders and stares into me. "Letting him grow up." He leans over and hugs me, hard. "I have never been as proud as I am right now."

"Ugh! Come with me, Martin." Mom turtles her hand into her sleeve, and once germ-protected, reaches for my arm. "We have some sanitizing to do."

I step back. "Thanks. But I think I'll just grab a shower."

My father is proud of me. My heart will burst. A happy burst. I can endure it all — the curse, the everything. I jog up the stairs and into the bathroom, my life suddenly full. I check my back, marvel at the stripe of red Poole gave me, and feel a grin.

"What I said in jail? I don't mean it. I am thankful for everything."

CHAPTER 23

Martin! Where've you been? I've found out so much about ancient curses and we have to talk!" Julia pages through her notebook. "Take this one. King Tut's curse. A guy named Howard Carter opened the pharaoh's tomb. But his exploring buddy died of a mosquito bite weeks later. Some reports even say a snake ate his canary! But Howard survived, so that was a 50/50 deal."

I lean back against the lockers and let my head fall back with a thud. "You wouldn't believe it, Julia. Not in a million years."

She shifts on her feet. "Try me."

"Well—"

The bell dongs and we all move toward first period. "Are you coming to the track meet tonight?"

"I have to. Detention. Remember?"

"Okay. Poole's coming and I'll talk to Charley. I think it's time to schedule one last OSM meeting."

"What do you mean 'one last'?" She clenches her jaw. "There's not going to be a last. You have to think positive."

I say nothing. She shoves my shoulder and stomps off. *Think positive.*

The day goes by slowly, which is fine by me. I'm in no mood to hurdle. The day also goes by differently. Mr. Halden, Gladys Gladys, even Will — they all make me smile. I'd invite all three of them over for a party if it would buy me more time. But it won't. Nothing will.

The school day ends, and I march to the locker room. I change for track and slowly walk out to the field.

"Where you been the last two days?" Charley runs up behind me while I stretch out on the track. "You get a paper cut?"

I roll my eyes, drop down, and stretch my skinny calves. "I went to work with Dad."

"No way. At the fort?"

Loudspeakers blare, "All non-competitors please clear the track!"

"That's me," he says. "Good luck, Marty."

"Yeah. Can you do another midnight meeting on Saturday?"

"Will Julia be there?"

"She's invited," I say.

"Count me in. Gotta go."

I watch him run off toward the stands. Slow of mind, but no worries. Julia sits in her regular corner. Dad and Mom watch from the other side. Well, Dad watches. Mom lathers the metal bleachers with liquid disinfectant. A ten-foot empty space has formed around my parents on the otherwise crowded bleachers.

And it hits. As I stare at her, a new feeling grows. Not anger. Pity. I feel sorry for her, trapped inside her paranoid skin. I lie back and stretch my back, stare into clear blue sky. I was like that. No more. I've just found one of death's perks.

I glance around the field. School buses from around St. Paul line up outside the fence surrounding the track, and runners cover the lanes. My first track meet is a huge event, and teammates go crazy. I should at least cheer when Midway wins, but I can't bring myself to hype more than a clap.

"Hurdles. 300 meters!"

"Let's go, Martin." Coach calls. The team is freaky excited and lines the inside of the track.

I peek up at Julia and she waves. I'm suddenly nervous. Dad smiles down on me, and my butterflies turn to small birds.

Might be my last chance. Win the tournament and I receive my father's coat of arms, his seal of approval. And I impress the lady. A knight is humble, faithful, and expects nothing in return. Ah, the agony of courtly love.

I lower my gaze, stretch my thighs, and march to the starting blocks. I will win. For all the things that could have been, I will —

"Oh my."

Other hurdlers mill about around the start. They are not boys. They are man-boys. Their bodies are huge, with furry upper lips and chins. They are beasts, not children, with thighs like tree trunks.

I step into lane three and stare down the track. Surrounded by Goliaths, I now only want the hurdles behind me.

I peek at the monster to my right. He sneers and licks his lips.

I reach into my pocket to make sure my chess horse is still there. Sure could use a real one right now.

I'm a knight. I'm a blistering-fast knight. I'm an … unhairy, under-developed, blistering-fast knight. I have faced hideous creatures and hideous curses and sharp-toothed jackals.

"Hey, monster. Are you really thirteen?"

Sasquatch grunts. I guess so. We put our feet in the blocks and our fingertips on the line. We're tense, like arrows on a string, ready to fly. Muscles ripple around me. At the slightest noise, my competition will launch, leaving me in their wake. Suddenly, I remember my vow.

"I'm thankful I'm not furry!"

Every other hurdler leaps forward.

"False start, lane 1 ... uh, and 2, 4, 5, and 6."

The Furry Ones growl and return to their positions. One more false start and they'll be disqualified.

"Sorry guys. I didn't mean to startle you. I just had to get that out —" A grin works its way across my face.

We lean over.

"Abubalah!" I scream.

"False start lane 1. Runner disqualified."

One man-boy is out of the race.

"Zeebobie! Gooba! Tooby Toby!"

Lane 2, 5, and 6 leap too soon, furry victims of my stupid-word strategy. The beast in lane 4 glares at me. It's down to Sasquatch and me.

"Heebeegeebee!" he yells, and I jump.

"Got me, monster." I tap my temple. We grunt at each other.

"Foobee!" I shout.

"Weeboowaaba!" he hollers.

"Doopee!"

"Mameemoo!"

The starter looks confused, shrugs, and fires.

The beast charges ahead. I follow, hollering, "Geenowa! Flapeeapee!"

He loses his step and plows through a hurdle, then tumbles to the ground. I leap past.

"Herky Dweeb!" he shouts.

I laugh and don't even jump the next hurdle. "Smowee! Kemaapa!"

The beast and I stagger forward, tears filling our eyes, crashing into every hurdle. We knock over the last ones and bend over, grabbing our guts. The finish line is just feet away. I pull his ear toward my mouth and whisper, "Merp."

He crumples into a laughing heap, and I shuffle across the finish line.

The announcer is silent. The crowd is silent. I raise my fists and Loudspeaker Man breaks out of his trance.

"The winner of the 300 meter hurdles: Martin Boyle of Midway Middle School."

The crowd erupts. Dad cheers. Mom frowns. Julia and Poole laugh.

It's a great day.

"I'm going to celebrate with the team."

I hate lying to Dad. I hate it. But I don't know how else to get free. Family and friends circle me in the Midway parking lot. Lani grabs my hand and squeezes. She knows something; I see it in her worried face.

"That was using your head to win a race." Dad pats my back. "Never seen that before."

"And you never shall again." Mom wipes her hands clean with antibac towelettes. "Every time your body came in contact with a hurdle, millions of germs and parasites leaped onto you."

"But those little critters didn't slow down our son." Dad rounds Mom's shoulder and squeezes. "Did they?"

Mom peeks at Dad, softens. "No, they didn't."

Dad smiles. "Into the car, Elaina. Lani?"

Sis doesn't let me go, and Dad tugs gently on her shoulders. I force a smile, release my grip, and her hand slips free. Lani climbs in, presses her nose and a hand against the glass. I press the window from the other side, the dying side, until the Suburban pulls away, leaving me with Poole and Julia. I stare at Poole. "Frank's okay with this?"

"As long as you don't jump out."

Julia frowns at Poole, then turns to me. "What's going on?"

"Can you call Lucy and tell her you need to go to Charley's?" I ask.

"Well, yeah." She pulls out her cell. "I do that all the time now."

Poole grabs Julia and me by the arm. "What are we waiting for? Your chariot awaits."

Frank's truck is parked behind the buses. We tumble in and clunk twenty minutes down the highway. Fresh off a victory and surrounded by friends, the horror doesn't seem possible, and I relax.

"We're here," I say.

Julia squints out the window. "Hot Air Balloon Rides of the St. Croix Valley. Really? We get to go up?"

I raise my eyebrows. "Two thousand dollars means we can do whatever we want."

"You mind the balloon folk, hear? Mind me too." Frank hops out of the truck. "The last time I was a daddy, my *son* caused quite a stir at school. My kids need to be obedient. Follow."

We enter the building, and Frank fills out waivers for both of us. Once done, he turns to leave. "I'll be sleeping in the truck. Martin, no fighting with your sister."

"What about prune—"

"No fighting."

My new sister and I walk through the building to where baskets and balloons are tethered. Soon the gas blower has a beautiful blue balloon tugging at the earth. I help Julia into the basket.

"You need your backpack?" I ask.

She nods her head. We sit down while our pilot lifts the balloon into the sunset. In no time, we're one thousand feet up. It's cold, and we huddle beneath a wool blanket.

"It was a great race today," she says.

I don't answer.

"What's wrong?" She quiets. "Dumb question."

I peek at her. "There are so many things I waited to do until now. There's a lot I won't get to do. Look."

The sky ripples pinks and purples and we're a part of it. Far below our shadow stretches long across the St. Croix.

Julia presses into my shoulder. "Don't give up. I can't think of that." She reaches for her pack. "You need to see this."

She removes her portfolio. "What I showed you before were sketches, while you kept adding installments. Now I think I'm up to date."

I flip open the portfolio and gasp.

They might not be as pretty as the sky, but they come close. A jackal in mid-shape shift, the escape from the cemetery, Alia — looking more like Julia with each new scene — peering out from the cave.

"What happened here?" I run my finger over two splotches near the bottom of the cave. "Looks like you spilled — "

"I cried, okay?" She snatches her art back. "I cried a little doing that one."

I nod. "That's okay. I've done that a few times too." Squirming over, I take the knight from my pocket and set it on my knee.

"You still have it!" She reaches up and strokes the tiny mane.

"I just wish I had two and that they were real and we could ride — at least you'll have Poole to keep you company."

She smacks my arm. "What does that mean?"

"I just thought since you two seem to get along, you'd end up friends, or ..."

Julia bursts into tears. I don't know what I said. I don't know why talking about Poole makes her cry. I don't know anything.

We land in a field on a perfect night. I hop out of the basket. Julia sulks, slumped down with arms crossed. She's not moving.

"I've spent tons of time looking up curses," she murmurs, staring straight ahead. "But since you've already given up, I guess that was a waste of time. I guess you're a waste of time."

I watch the chase crew's van approach in the distance. Soon we're zipping back towards Frank's truck.

"Howdy, kids!" Frank offers his biggest toothless grin. "How was the stratosphere?"

Julia walks past his words, hops in the truck, and slams the door. I mope behind her.

Poole jumps into the truck bed, and Frank squeezes behind the wheel. "Didn't I speak to you two about fighting?" He starts the ignition.

Julia tongues her cheek and mutters, "You should have spoken to him about quitting."

CHAPTER 24

DAYS PASS QUICKLY. JULIA IS NOT IN SCHOOL. MY mind hazes and my body sweats. Something deep inside is happening. Something horrible and unstoppable.

The curse accelerates.

"She won't come to our OSM meeting." I climb on top of the locomotive beside Poole and take in the morning. It's beautiful.

He whacks the metal roof with a stick. "Oh, I bet she will. She likes you."

"She hates me. She won't talk to me."

"That proves it." He pokes me with his stick. "That's how it works."

I wipe wet off my forehead and stare at the rising sun. "It's not so much the dying. It's the leaving. I don't want to leave her or Dad or grimy you ... or Lani and Mom."

"Wait until tonight." He leans over and bumps my shoulder. "Wait until the meeting. You ain't gone yet."

I spend all of Saturday in my bedroom — anxious, waiting. When I come out for lunch, Mom stares at me and smiles.

"How nice to see you looking as you did before. I was worried you'd lost your general good sense."

I want to talk to her. I want her to be a mom just once and not a crazy woman.

"Do you ever get afraid? Do you ever think about something that's coming up and wish you could blow the day back on the calendar, but you know you can't? You know the Big Scary is coming. Do you ever wish you could do that?"

Mom plops mashed potatoes on my plate. "No, Martin. I do not fear, for I plan. I plan for every emergency. Then nothing catches me off guard." She pauses. "It's a — well, your father would say it's a heavy way to live and he might be correct, but once the habit is formed, well, no use talking about this. I'll get the gravy."

She disappears into the kitchen and does not reappear. I don't need gravy. I don't need food. I rise and reach for the stairway rail. I haul myself higher, stagger into my room, and collapse against the door. My heart thumps slowly and loudly, and I try to catch my breath, but it's no use.

"In, out. In, out," I whisper, and work my lungs like an accordion. *Can't just sit here.*

My story sits on my chair. I lunge for the tablet. "Okay, the centipede told the knight that the princess went back to the magic fort." I prop myself up on an elbow.

"I won't catch her on foot. To the air. I must find … Hallo!"

Before the knight, the skies grew dark, and a spindly finger dropped to the earth. The twister jumped and danced, sucking a herd of cows high into the swirling clouds.

"Storm! I need transport!"

"To what end?" Its thunderous voice shook the ground.

"My princess flees to danger, to the Black Knight's lair."

The storm roared. "That accursed knight! Prepare yourself. Sheath your sword."

The White Knight obeyed, bowed, and swirled heavenward. Faster he spun, his hands clenching his weapon.

"Godspeed," thundered the wind, and the knight spun to the ground. His sight blurred and his feet staggering from the twister's twirling…

I blink hard. The words on the paper blur, and nausea sweeps over me. I have no strength. Hours before the meeting in the boxcar, I'm fading fast. I lie down on the bedroom rug — the bed is too far away — and fall asleep.

Eyelids shoot open.

Plink. Plink.

Small stones ricochet off my window glass. I glance at the time. 12:10 a.m.

"Late!" I jump to my feet, grab a chair to steady myself, and tiptoe down the stairs. On the last step my legs give way, and I tumble to the floor.

So this is how it is.

I crawl to the boxcar. Poole, Charley, and Julia all poke out their heads.

"How are we supposed to save you if you don't show up?" Poole reaches down and pulls me into the car.

"Sorry. I — It's getting hard to move."

I crumple into a chair. "Have you started without me?"

"No," says Julia. She grins. "Not without you."

"I may as well go first," I say. "Fort Snelling was a bust. There was a Martin Boyle. He was one of the first soldiers there." I exhale hard. "I spent some time in jail with a guy who knew him, or at least a guy who was pretending to be a guy who knew him. It's all so confusing."

"Go on, Marty." Poole kneels down in front of me.

"He said he was the mason. He said he carved the cornerstone with my name on it — "

"Stop!" Julia jumps up. "Okay. Curses in the 1800s. Here's what I know. Yeah, people said them, but if they really wanted to make them stick, they would chisel them into something permanent. Permanent words, permanent curse." Her face glows and she clears her throat.

"1839. London. One James Davies hired a Gerald Rothchild, tombstone engraver, to engrave tombstones for himself and his wife, Louisa. After the work was completed, and the tombstones set in the graveyard, without the death date, of course ..."

"Of course," I say.

Julia continues, "Mr. Davies tells Mr. Rothchild he cannot pay him for his work. Mr. Rothchild is so angry, he goes to the cemetery and carves 1839 as the death year for Mr. and Mrs. Davies. Sure enough, two months later, the Davies both drowned in the North Sea ... So! If you find that cornerstone, you might find — "

"Nothing." Poole glances at her. "I did see it. The only names on there were James Delaney and William Goddard. No message. No curse."

We don't speak for minutes.

Charley's been pacing, his hands pushing through his hair. He stops. "I don't want you to die."

He's almost crying. I don't know what to do. Julia is misty and Poole's at my feet and Charley is crying. I force my way vertical and stumble toward him. He holds up his hand.

"No. You stay there. You stay right there and you don't die 'cause this is stupid. Nobody dies because of curses. Especially you. Because I hate you." He jumps

out of the boxcar. "I hate you for leaving me. I hate you."
He runs into the night. "I hate you!"

I back onto the couch, bury my face in my hands,
and whisper, "You're the best, Charley."

I spread my fingers and peek through at Julia. She
rests her head on my shoulder. "When is your aunt supposed to, you know?"

"A week. Her due date is in one week." I lift my arm
and watch it flop onto my lap. "That race stole all the
energy I had. I don't know how I'll make it until then.
It's tough to walk now."

Poole hops up. "One week. Seven days. One hundred sixty-eight hours. That's a lot of time. We can do
this."

I stand. "I'm so tired. OSM is over." I slide out of
the boxcar.

"Julia was right, ya quitter!" Poole yells at my back.
He might be right. But I've had a great three months and
how am I supposed to fight a curse?

"Keep on walkin'! You lazy, good-for-nothing—"

I slam the front door on his anger. I should be the
angry one, but I'm not, for some reason I'm not. Maybe
it's all that thankfulness. Maybe I'm delusional. But
seems to me I've been given a pretty good life.

CHAPTER
25

"DAD, WHAT ARE YOU DOING UP?"

He sits in his seldom-used main-floor den. Usually he's retreated into Underwear World by now.

Dad beams. "It's an exciting night. Landis just called from the hospital. Can you imagine Landis in a hospital? I'm surprised he knew how to use the phone."

My heartbeat flutters. "Is he okay?"

"He wanted a home birth, but sometimes babies surprise a man."

"Babies." I swallow hard. "But it's too early."

Dad grabs my shoulders. "You're going to have a cousin, likely by morning. I'm waiting now for word." He cocks his head. "You're pale, Martin. Really pale. Go get some rest. It'll be a full day at the hospital tomorrow."

He swirls his back to me and goes to work on the computer. I turn to leave.

"Oh, and one more thing," he says. "What did you spend your college money on?"

It doesn't matter now. "Hot air balloon ride. But most of it's still in my middle desk drawer. Feel free."

"Was it fun?"

"Until the fighting part."

His fingers fly over the keyboard. "I need to know I can trust you, Martin. No more withdrawals from the account, agreed?"

"Believe me, no more."

What's the best way to die? Alone? Flopping lifeless in front of your parents? Lani should not see it, that's for sure.

I haul up the steps, grab my story from my bedroom, and keep going down the hall. I climb into the attic. It's cold and damp, sort of how I feel.

I pull the chain on the light bulb and sit in the chair in the center of the attic. And wait.

This waiting will drive me crazy!

I grab my notebook from beneath the chair, set my chess knight in front of me, and sigh. This all started as a story for Julia. I need to finish it.

The White Knight ... no, that's not his name. I take a shallow breath. It's me.

I ran toward the fortress and across the lowered draw-bridge. There, in the center of the courtyard, was a stone gnarled like wood and old like a mountain. It towered so high its peak poked above the walls. I stared into it, and gasped. Two eyes stared out. Grayish, tormented eyes. The eyes of the princess. Julia was trapped once again, but in none of the beauty or brilliance of the clear stone. She looked old, tired, and bent, as if this tomb had sucked all the youth from her bones.

"Is she not a sorry sight?"

The Black Knight appeared from behind the rock of death, his minions rising as one on top of fortress walls.

"She is nothing to me now." The Black Knight stroked the scar on his cheek. "Prepare to taste death together." He squinted and snarled. "And to think you fancy yourself a hero."

A force inescapable took hold of me, my strength vanished, and I walked resolutely toward the rock. I knew my fate. I would reach the boulder, enter it, and all hope would be lost.

The Black Knight laughed. "Do you not like my rock? With my own hands I carved your forever home. To think I learned my craft at your father's side. Such tragic irony."

"Black Knight, Dark Counselor, Evil Creature. Now that you've won. Pray tell. What is your name?" I asked.

The Black Knight grew grim. "No, heir. That will forever be my secret. Do you not know that words have power?"

I slam the book shut. "That's twice, Poole, twice that you've weaseled your way into my story."

A wave of panic washes over me. *I don't want to be alone.*

I grab my little knight and stumble down the stairs. Dad sits where I left him. I slip in the den and ease down. "Dad?"

He jumps and spins in his chair. His eyes narrow. "You look even worse."

I nod. "I just wanted to say that I think you're a great dad and ... thank you."

"For what?" He folds his arms and gives his penetrating look.

"Um, well, for taking me to the fort. That was kind of fun, actually."

"You surprised me," Dad smiles. "I was very impressed with how you carried yourself. A real soldier." He locks his fingers behind his head and leans back. "Next time we won't let the Colonel keep us from exploring around the fort."

I open my mouth to tell him everything, but I can't. "Okay."

"There's a lot to see. You'll enjoy the adventure more now that you understand the proud name you bear."

I squint. "My proud name?"

"Didn't James tell you all about the first Martin's exploits? You were in jail together, weren't you?"

"James the crazy drunk stonemason? He was —"

"Your great-great-great-great-great-grandfather's

neighbor at the fort. An eyewitness to the first Martin's bravery." Dad winks. "And the actor who plays him, well, he's also a childhood friend of mine. He's perfect for the role. One, he actually works with stone, and two, his name really is James. He used to chisel little wooden figures, and I'd blow them up. We terrorized our neighborhood."

I rewind *The White Knight* in my mind and hit the play button.

The Black Knight laughed. "Do you not like my rock? With my own hands I carved your forever home. To think I learned my craft at your father's side. Such tragic irony."

Whoa! James grew up at my dad's side.

Dad continues, "James and I joined Fort Snelling's reenactment infantry on the same day." He shakes his head. "You owe him more than you realize."

"What do I owe him?"

"You came into this world a few weeks early. It was my last day stationed at Fort Hood. Your mother was here and needed to get to the hospital. James showed up on the doorstep. What a good friend."

The king trusted the Black Knight. Dad trusted James …

"Yeah." My mouth goes dry. "So your friend was at the hospital. Think he could have grabbed my toe?"

Dad frowns. "Your toe?"

James was there at my birth! But wait, Dad's friend can't be the Black Knight; he's alive now. He couldn't curse all the Martins before me . . .

A bead of sweat traces down my cheek. "Forget it. If he's such a good friend, why haven't I seen him?"

"Something changed after you were born. We grew apart." Dad lowers his voice. "Still, we work together at the fort, and I figured he would fill you in on the first Martin's heroics while you two were in the Guard House."

"Heroics?"

"Our ancestor saved that camp." Dad stares into the distance. "Ah, the first Martin Boyle. There can only be one Martin."

A knife-like pain jabs my stomach, and I groan.

"Son, are you — "

"Keep talking, please."

Dad frowns. "A famous story, really. So back in 1820, the original James Delaney was so thankful to Martin for saving so many men and women and children, he carved him a memorial stone, after Martin had died, of course. The fort actually considered the rock its cornerstone."

"No." I wipe sweat off my forehead. "Poole saw the cornerstone in the Fort. There's no mention of me, I mean the other Martin."

Dad rolls his eyes. "What do they teach in school

these days? Son, when the Fifth Regiment, the one that built the fort, first arrived at the site of what is now Fort Snelling, what did they see?"

"Uh—"

"That's right. Nothing. Grass and trees. There was no Fort Snelling. Through that first, harsh winter, during construction, where did they stay?"

"Uh. Somewhere else?"

"Yes. Somewhere else. New Hope Cantonment."

My eyes widen. "Another fort."

"Another fort." Dad smiles. "Temporary. A place to store the materials and men while they built Fort Snelling. And *that's* where Martin saved half the regiment by his heroic trade missions. Sickness hit. Most of the men died. Many women died. Martin's firstborn son died. But he alone kept bringing in food he got from the Indians. He was so sick, but he tramped mile after mile after mile. And then he died."

Dad stands and walks to the bookshelf. "I usually only take this down for our cemetery gathering." He opens a weathered book. "But read for yourself. The account written by the first Martin's widow."

My vision blurs, and I blink hard and reach for the book.

My Martin's last words before he left me forever: Don't worry about the boy or me. I swear this on our lives; there will always be one Martin in this family. And one is enough.

"Blek!" I cry. "The first Martin said that?" The stench of curseness. I read on.

The men have taken my Martin's words and rallied around the courage they express. James seems uniquely affected, as 'There Will Only be One Martin Boyle' is now scrawled on the commemorating cornerstone resting in the middle of the camp.

"Double blek! It gets worse. Thanks a lot, James. Permanent words, permanent curse!"

I jump to my feet.

That's the beginning. The beginning of the end of all the Martins.

The beginning of the end of me!

The first Martin and his neighbor did it to us all!

"Where are you going?" asks Dad.

I close my eyes, imagine a pencil in my hand, and write.

"Words have power!"

"You're a stonemason," I whispered. "Your name. Your name is James. Not Knight, not Counselor. You are James!"

"Silence!" James flew into a rage and charged toward me, his sword raised.

Behind me, a hideous sound. The jackal pounced over my head and sunk his teeth into James's raised arm. The two rolled around on the ground. I tried to stop, but still I walked.

"Down! Down here!"

Below my feet, a centipede raced to match my morbid march.

"How did you—"

"Look down, before the rock grew, toward the bottom, when time began. Look down here. What do you see?"

I took another step toward the rock and squinted at the base. "I see scratchings. Words."

"Destroy them!" yelled the centipede. "You've found the cornerstone. Words have power."

Like Julia said. Find that cornerstone.

The phone rings and my eyelids fly open. Dad answers. "In labor? Congratulations! Get back in there and be of some help."

He hangs up. "You're going have a cousin in a matter of hours. What do you think about that?"

"I think the first Martin accidentally spoke a curse on all the Martins born after him, and then the Black Knight, a.k.a Mr. James Delaney, a.k.a his grateful neighbor, a.k.a the drunk mason, set the curse in stone!" My legs weaken, and I grab the back of my chair. "I think I have two hours to do what Julia and the centipede say and destroy the rock, if I can find it."

I push out the door, pause and turn. "And you really need to choose your friends more carefully."

Dad frowns. "Get some sleep, please."

"Yeah," I run out the garage door, grab the sledgehammer, and drag it into the night. "Be there, Poole. Be there." I race around the side of the house and exhale hard. A dull light still glows from inside the boxcar. I approach and hear Poole and Julia.

"Hey! Poole! I need you. We have two hours. Can you get us to Fort Snelling in two hours?"

He pokes his head out. "Done! Come on."

Julia jumps down and lifts the sledgehammer from my hands. "What's this?"

"My sword."

CHAPTER 26

IT'S A DARK NIGHT, FULL OF FOG AND MIST. I SLUMP against the back of the boxcar, my forehead on fire. My body jars to the rhythm of the rails, and I stare out at city lights racing by.

Julia and Poole speak quietly near the train car's mouth. Every so often she looks over her shoulder and smiles. But it looks forced and doesn't last long.

"How much longer?" I ask, and break into a coughing spell.

Poole waits for me to finish. "Twenty minutes, maybe thirty."

I press my head against the cold metal. The cool feels good. Closing my eyes does too.

"Marty. Come on!" Poole's face blurs. "We have one minute to get off." Poole reaches under my shoulder and yanks. "We're here."

"Here." I swallow hard. "Where's that?"

"Fort Snelling." Julia grabs my other shoulder.

I swallow hard. "That's nice. My dad works here, you know."

We hobble to the edge and I tumble out, wobble like the world. "Fort Snelling! We need to hurry. My sword, where is it?"

"Leave it, friend." Poole takes hold of my arm.

"No!" I try to climb back in, but my leg slips. Julia jumps up and drags out the sledgehammer.

"I have your ... sword."

Together we hurry out of the station. It's a strange kind of hurry. Three shadows stumbling through the mist. It's hard to see anything, but after ten minutes, the imposing shape of Fort Snelling rises in the distance.

"Okay, centipede, where to?" I whisper.

"Hold it!"

A husky voice yells from the fort and we freeze. The front gate springs to life with shouts and movement.

"Go!" Poole hisses. "Whatever you got to do, move quick."

"But I don't know where to look." I glance around. "Some other fort. There's some other fort, or there was or should be or — "

Poole shoves me behind a tree. "Move!" He jumps out and walks toward the Gatehouse. "Look by the river. They always built stuff by rivers. They were like roads or train tracks." He pauses. "Learned that when you sent me to school. Now if you'll excuse me, I have a fort to attack."

Julia helps me to my feet.

"Hallo, spooky soldier guys! I'm a little lost." Poole calls. "Anyone seen the Midway train depot?"

His shadow disappears in a host of sentry shadows, who hustle him through the gate. The night outside returns to quiet.

Whatever happens to me, I'm thankful for you, Poole.

"Help me up." I say.

Julia grabs me by the arm. "You're cold. Really cold."

"To the river." I point to my sledgehammer. "You'll have to lug that. I'll manage."

Together we stagger through the woods, twigs and brush snapping beneath our feet.

"Problem is ..." I gasp for air. "Fort Snelling sits on two rivers. I don't know which one to search along."

"Minnesota."

Julia screams, and I tumble to the ground.

"Didn't think I sounded that frightening." Squirrel reaches out a hand. "You don't look so good. You should see Dr. Kearney in the infirmary."

"I should not! I need to find New Hope Cantonment. Do you know where that is?"

"Where it was. We don't need it anymore. We have Fort—"

"Squirrel!"

"Fine. I was just giving some history. You realize I didn't have to listen to your friend or come find you." He straightens. "Who's this?"

"I'm Julia."

"It's a pleasure to — "

"Squirrel," I gasp. "Please."

He clears his throat. "Fine. We'll proceed without proper introduction." Squirrel takes the lead and veers to the right. "It's a half mile from here. We should be there soon."

"You're going to make it," whispers Julia.

I swallow hard and walk on. I feel less with each step. The branches that scratch me, the cool mist on my skin. I feel less. The world and me are saying good-bye. Only Julia seems more. I'm not in this alone. I glance at the hammer. She holds the handle with both hands and drags it behind her through the woods. She's carrying my load.

Beep!

Squirrel whips around. "What in tarnation — "

"My cell. Sorry." Julia digs it out, peeks from the phone to me. "It's your mom. Charley must've caved under pressure. My foster mom probably found me gone, called his place and found out I was at your place, and your mom, well, what should I do?"

"Here." I slide open the case and take a deep breath. "Hey, Mom, I can't talk now. I'm okay. Well, not really okay, but I'm not in danger so I'm okay that way but that doesn't matter. What matters is that I want to tell you I love ya, 'cause I do even if you're kind of over the top sometimes or all the time. It doesn't matter anymore. But I love you and I'll see you — well, I love ... Bye, Mom."

I suck in a lungful of air as Mom's voice cuts into the night. "Come home now! Landis called. Should be any — "

I slide the cell cover closed. Julia and I stare at the phone.

"Hurry, Squirrel."

We pick up the pace, a lumbering, falling, fearsome pace. The sound of water rushes in front of us.

"Almost there." Squirrel breaks out of the trees and runs for the bank. Julia lets go of me, hoists the hammer, and leaps out after. I shuffle out, my legs noodling. All sensations fire. Like in Mr. Halden's Treatment.

"This is it." Squirrel runs around the grassy field. "You are standing in New Hope Cantonment."

"But there's nothing here!" Julia grabs Squirrel and shakes. "Nothing but high grass."

"I told you, we don't need it anymore."

Ring.

My replacement is coming. I feel energy drain from my head, then my shoulders. It drains into the ground. I was wrong. I took a chance and listened to a stupid centipede and now Julia will have to watch another person die.

Ring.

That's the call. Martin's here. Answer the phone and I'm done.

"Martin! What should I do?"

"Don't answer." I step forward, my foot catches, and I fall face-first. My arms don't even try to break impact. I smash into the earth. Funny, it doesn't hurt. I'm glad it won't hurt.

Ring.

The phone sounds like it's a mile away. I'm on my back. Julia's face is dropping tears onto mine. She's speaking. It's muddled. My head lifts. Both her and Squirrel lift my noodle and prop it on a rock. I blink. I tripped over a rock. I'm on a rock.

Inscription. Cornerstone. Rock.

"Anything … written … on this rock?" I wheeze.

Julia has the flashlight. She wipes her eyes and shines the beam over my face. It blinds me.

"It says … It says ONLY — Squirrel, what does that — It says ONLY — "

Ring.

"ONLY ONE. It says ONLY ONE."

There will only be one Martin.

"Sword," I rasp. "I need … to smash this stone!"

Julia lunges for it.

"Squirrel, get my head off this; prop me up. And Julia … the hammer."

"You can't hold it!" she yells. "Tell me what to do!"

"I have to do it. It has to be me."

Ring.

I float, lifted slowly up into the fog. Below me, I watch myself kneeling down in front of the rock, my hands shaking violently on the handle of the hammer. Julia stands behind me, lifting the heavy end of the sledgehammer into the air. Squirrel stands back. It's a nice view, but the figures are getting smaller. I reach into my pocket. The knight is gone.

I fear this was meant to be. Mom's voice echoes through my skull.

"Let. Go. Julia," I say, my words floating up soft and muddled.

Far beneath me, the metal head falls. The rock explodes into shards of light, and I feel a fist, strong like gravity, squeeze the air out of me. I'm gasping. I can't breathe, and I hurtle back down toward the earth. I land with a thud, a thud I feel, and the fist releases. Air fills my lungs, and the night fills with Julia's sobs.

"Martin! It's not fair. It's not."

Ring.

I crack an eyelid. "Answer it."

"What? You're okay? Answer it?" She flings open her phone, and her voice quavers. "Hello?"

"Wah!" One hundred percent pure baby.

"Ya hear that?" asks Landis. "Is Martin there?"

I slowly reach for the phone.

"It's Landis. What do you think about these lungs? Here, listen!"

"Wah!"

"Pretty doggone impressive, and Jenny — she just pushed the little critter right — ow, honey! I was just tellin' the boy about the process. Sorry, Marty. Jenny smacked me. But I figured you should hear the boy first. Didn't want you to think you'd be the last Martin."

I grin. And the grin turns bigger and then works its way inside, where it gathers momentum and bursts out in a laugh strong and free. I laugh and laugh and don't know why I laugh but I can't stop it. Landis laughs and in the background Jenny laughs and in front of me Julia laughs.

And faintly now, the next Martin cries.

I stand up, my body full of strength and my hands full of shattered stones. One by one, they skip into the river, which quickly carries away the ripples.

What do you do when someone hits the redo button on your life and you get a chance to start all over? What should you do first?

I stare at Julia, her tears falling across a smile, and I know where to begin.

POSTSCRIPT

I unsheathed my sword and swung. The blade nicked the rock, and for a moment all was still.

Softly, like a series of snapping twigs, a thin crack snaked its way up to the peak, and then with deafening thunder, the gnarled stone mountain crashed to the ground. Dust settled and the air cleared.

The Black Knight and his followers had fled.

I stared at the mound that was to have been my tomb. I smiled. There would be no death for me today.

But Julia!

"Martin?" Her voice rang clear from the within the heap.

I scampered up the rocks, casting them aside and calling as I climbed. "Julia! Are you sound?"

"Yes." Her words held no pain, and I scanned the castle grounds. "Jackal, Centipede, lend me a paw. And a foot. The princess lives!"

The centipede crawled into a crack in the stones and emerged moments later. "By rights, my Lady should be crushed, but she sits in a hollow, the rock domed about her."

"Free her!" I shouted.

The ground shook and I stared at the jackal. "What evil comes?"

"None, sire. The Black Knight's power is broken. And without his strength, the castle will soon crumble like the stone." He paused. "Listen. The moat, it rises. Magic no longer contains the river that once flowed near this stronghold. Dig quickly!"

I threw rocks to the left and right as water poured into the courtyard.

"Hurry, Martin!" Julia cried. "The water; it rises."

I can't. There's no way I'll reach her in time.

I collapsed on the stones. "We've come so far. It cannot end this way."

"And it shall not!"

From behind me, a trumpet blast. An army on horseback splashed over the drawbridge, with my father, King Gav the Brave, at the lead. He reached the mound and leaped off his steed. The king climbed to my side and I began to bow, but my father reached down and lifted my head.

"When last I saw you, perhaps a fitting gesture, but no longer. Stand straight, my son. I am proud of you."

The jackal tugged at my father's leg.

"Tas! My old friend." My father knelt down eye level with the creature. "What strange fortune brings you—"

"If I may be so bold, we have not the time for greetings. Water rushes in, my lord."

My father nodded and rose. "Martin, where is this girl?"

I pointed beneath his feet.

"Warriors!" he cried. "Barricade the gate. Divert the flood—"

"Wait." I grabbed his arm. "Time has indeed changed me. Julia is mine to save."

The king smiled and handed me his sword. "My army awaits your command."

I raised the blade. "Clear the stone!"

As one, the men fell upon the rubble. They tossed chunks of stone into the torrent, now lapping their waists. I bent down on the pile and pushed slabs off the top. They tumbled into the rising water with a splash.

Suddenly, from within the pile, a beam of light pierced my eyes. Rock near my feet shifted and caved in on itself, leaving a gaping hole.

"Julia!"

I reached down through the opening, felt her hand grasp mine, and pulled. Soon she stood at my side, her face clear and whole.

Again, the ground shook.

"Away, men. Away!" I yelled.

Father's men tried to mount, but the river, just released, held a fury of its own. King Gav sounded his trumpet. "Release your horses. We must climb!"

I grabbed Julia's hand and we leaped off the mound, pushed through the current, and reached the stairs. We scaled and sputtered and soon stood atop the castle walls. I gazed into the courtyard. Only the crumbled peak remained above the water line.

Julia drew close. "Will we survive?"

I sighed. "I do not know how high the water will rise."

"No, Martin. Now that your curse is broken. Will you and I survive? Or will you leave me to live life alone?" Worry creased her face. "You've done this before."

I faced Julia and—

"Psst. Martin."

I look up and smile. Poole's head pops through my open window.

"It's a beautiful night. In the mood for a stroll, friend? Hey. I thought you finished that story."

I exhale hard and close my notebook. "I thought so, too."